The Peacemaker

T. L. Criswell

The Peacemaker

T. L. Criswell

abbott press®

A DIVISION OF WRITER'S DIGEST

The Peacemaker

ISBN: 978-1-4582-0498-1 (sc)
ISBN: 978-1-4582-0499-8 (e)
ISBN: 978-1-4582-0500-1 (hc)

Library of Congress Control Number: 2012912519

Abbott Press books may be ordered through booksellers or by contacting:

Abbott Press
1663 Liberty Drive
Bloomington, IN 47403
www.abbottpress.com
Phone: 1-866-697-5310

Printed in the United States of America

Abbott Press rev. date: 05/29/2013

To my boys, Mehki, and Damon.
When you become an adult, I will gladly be your friend.
I love you both, more than words could ever express.

ACKNOWLEDGMENTS

First I want to give thanks to my creator; a higher power who has blessed me and filled my heart and soul with these words printed inside of this book. I want to thank my beautiful mother for giving me life and always believing in me.

I want to thank my husband, Mr. James Criswell, who is the love of my life. Thanks for loving me, inspiring me and believing in me. I will always cherish the day, over five years ago, when a complete stranger walked into our life and you opened up your heart and welcomed him in. Thank you for adopting my long lost nephew, Damon, and showing him unconditional love. You are the greatest husband, father, and friend. I appreciate you, and I am so proud to be your wife.

I want to send out big hugs and kisses to my one and only biological son, Mehki. I love you more than you will ever know. You are the center of my world, and I can't thank you enough for sharing me with your cousin, and step brothers.

A special thanks to my nephew, Damon Terrelle, who inspired me to finish this novel. I love you; you were truly heaven-sent!

To my step-sons, Jaron, and Keion, I want you to know that I love you both unconditionally.

Next I want to thank a person who taught me that just because you don't have a college degree doesn't mean you can't have a voice to offer to the world. Thanks for knowing how to meet people where they are, and thanks for helping me to use my creative mind without changing one word of this story. Ben Smith, I don't think that there is a word big enough to describe you, so I will settle for "brilliant." Thank you so much; you're the best.

Thanks to my BFF, Tamara Burnett, a great writer and one of the funniest people I have ever known. Thank you for always being there, especially when I needed a thought completed.

Special thanks to my sister, Tresa Brown, my brother, Terrance Parker, my sister in spirit Glenda Boyd, my aunt, Brenda Franklin and my cousin, Arnika Davis.

A special thanks to my Jefferson North family for all of your input, Kenyel Moore, Ricky McDaniel, Tawanna McGee, Kathy Bruen, Brenda Pasley, James Tucker and N. Robinson.

I cannot say thank you enough, to my aunt, Brenda Franklin, for always being there, and adding her special creative touch. Great job on designing the front cover of this book!

Much love,
T. L. Criswell

Contents

HUMILITY

My mind wanders to a world of its own when the slamming of the gate sends a jolt that penetrates my entire body, causing my head to throb. Officer Douglas stands before me, snapping his fingers and yelling my name. "Jayson Jackson," he calls, forcing me back into reality. "Spread 'em," he says in his usual loud, authoritative tone. I conform, all the while hoping that tomorrow my life will be my own.

My body stiffens as he pats me down under my arms and between my legs. This has been my life for over the past two years. I have tolerated this same form of humiliation on a weekly and sometimes daily basis, and it still doesn't get any easier. Being locked away from society has stripped me of my pride and dignity, and it's something that I can never grow accustomed to.

The officer turns the key, and the thick metal gate slowly opens. "One hour," he yells in a spiteful tone, being sure to inflict more pain on my already bruised ego.

My eyes quickly spot Nana on the other side of the visiting room. She is patiently waiting to restore as much of my dignity as she possibly can in that one hour, as she does every week.

I wave to Nana, but she doesn't wave back. Then I remember that my clean-cut appearance is quite different from what she has been used to seeing these past few years. My hair is no longer in a ponytail; it's cut short, and my mustache is gone, making me appear younger than my seventeen years. As I walk toward Nana, she looks noticeably different to me; offhand, I can't tell why.

When I stop and stand in front of Nana, she appears to be surprised. "Jayson, is that really you?"

"Yes! Nana, it's me," I answer bashfully.

"I love it," she says. "You look just like that ten-year-old little boy that I used to tuck in at night." she gives me a half smile. Nana is trying not to let on that she is worried, but she doesn't have to; it is written all over her face. I return the smile as I hold back my emotions, trying not to think about tomorrow, the day my life will change. Whether it will change for the better or the worse, it will change, and we both are afraid.

Nana reaches her thin arms out as I place my large, six-foot-two, 220-pound frame around her tiny body, and it feels as though I could swallow her whole. Although Nana stands at five foot two and weighs probably less than 100 pounds, she has always been the strongest woman in the world to me, and it hurts to see that she is weakening.

I arrange two chairs to face each other before I motion for her to sit down. Now that I am seated directly across from Nana, I am able to look deep into her eyes, and I become even more frightened by what I observe. Her caramel skin lacks her normal makeup; she looks pale. Her eyes are sad, and I attribute the large dark circles under them to a lack of sleep. Nana is also visibly shaking.

"Nana, are you all right?" Although I already know the answer, I feel it is the only appropriate thing to say.

She takes a deep breath and says, "I'm okay; just a little tired." I feel *horrible!* After everything that I have put her through, she still feels the need to protect me and my feelings. Of course she is tired; she hasn't had any sleep in over a week. How could she with every news station in the Detroit metropolitan area camped out in front of her house, determined to get an interview? Nana will not do it, however. She refuses to give an interview to anyone regarding me or my situation; she loves me far more than I deserve! When the entire community turned its back on me and labeled me a street thug, Nana came to my defense. "I don't care what these people accuse you of; I know who you are! You're still my grandson, and I will always love you, no matter what!" These were the words that she spoke to me the day that I was sentenced.

Nana never mentions the media to me, but she doesn't have to; I see it on the television. Last night I watched in horror as the news reporter said,

> We are standing in front of the home of Ms. Sarah Scott. She is the grandmother of Jayson Jackson II, the person who was tried and convicted of shooting Detroit's very own Mr. Basketball, Michael Stephens, two years

ago. This story made national headlines because Michael Stephens, a young boy raised by his grandmother on the east side of Detroit, didn't make his mark by turning to a life of crime and drugs like so many of his peers; he made his mark on the basketball court! As a result of winning Mr. Basketball, he received a full scholarship to Michigan State University. That dream wouldn't last long for Michael Stephens; it was stolen away in an instant with a single gunshot wound to the back. The shooter was Jayson Jackson.

The news reporter went on to say,

Jayson Jackson's attorney claimed that the shooting was accidental; but once he tested positive for drugs and alcohol the District Attorney's office didn't agree. They wanted justice for Michael and sought the prosecution of Jayson Jackson. Although Jayson Jackson was only fifteen at the time of the incident, the prosecutor wanted him tried as an adult.

Judge Rhonda Kemp sentenced him to two and a half years in a juvenile detention facility, and on his eighteenth birthday, the case will be up for review.

She continued by saying,

Well, that day has finally come! Tomorrow Jayson Jackson will be eighteen, and the judge could either let him walk free or give him a blended sentence, which would land him in a state correctional facility for a very long time. This shooting has shattered dreams, broken friendships, divided communities, and taken a personal toll on everyone who has followed this case.

I cut the television off after that; I no longer wanted to think about it.

I focus my attention back on Nana. "Nana, you shouldn't have come down here; you should have waited until tomorrow. Who brought you here anyway?"

She turns around and says, "Your Uncle Scott. He wanted me to have a talk with you before you stand in front of the judge tomorrow." My eyes roam the room, looking for Uncle Scott. I finally spot him in the very back, standing in front of the long picnic table and sorting through some papers, strategically organizing them in some sort of sequence.

Uncle Jeffery Scott is Nana's eldest child and my mother Jackie's brother. He is also my attorney, mentor, and friend (something that would have never happened on the outside world). Nana had pleaded with me to move with him to California before my troubles started, but I'd refused to go. (I regret that decision every day that I wake up in this place.)

Nana and I both walk over to the table where Uncle Scott is standing. He turns around and gives me a big, brotherly hug while Nana takes a seat at the table. After Uncle Scott and I finish with our embrace, he cuts to the chase and points his finger at the table.

"Jackson," he says, with a serious expression on his face, "study this table, and tell me, what you see?" The table is lined with pictures, and I begin to feel uncomfortable. The first one is of Michael and me at my seventh birthday party. We both are standing there next to Jackie, smiling as we hold up the peace sign. The next picture is of Michael and me fishing with Grandpa when we were about ten years old. The last picture is of us acting silly outside of Nana's house the summer before the accident. After looking at these pictures, I become choked up with emotion.

The next row contains at least ten different hurtful newspaper articles, along with my picture and several other juveniles' faces on the cover of one of the papers. The image is labeled, "Juvenile Violence ... How Do We Stop It?" My heart starts beating really fast.

"What's going through your mind, Jackson?" Uncle Scott says. I turn to look in the other direction because I am deeply saddened by the memories. Uncle Scott takes his hand and gently turns my face around so that I can read today's headlines. There is a picture of me on one side and Michael in full basketball uniform on the other; a bold line drawn straight down the middle divides the two of us. The headline reads, "Has Justice Been Served?" I'm mortified. The world will never forgive me, which makes it extremely difficult for me to forgive myself.

Again I try to turn away to escape the collage of memories from my past, but Uncle Scott won't let me off that easy. He rephrases the question: "Jackson, who am I looking at right now?" I swallow really hard. "The man that stands in front of me now—are you the same man that's lying on this table right here in these newspaper articles?" I know I am not that same man; I just don't know how to express myself to Uncle Scott.

He looks at me and reaches inside his briefcase. "I was afraid that you were not going to be able to answer these questions right away."

He hands me the paper, and before I get a chance to look at it, he asks another question. "Do you still blame your parents for the way that your life has turned out?" Once again, he doesn't give me a chance to answer the question before he asks another one. "Jackson, when you were first incarcerated, I asked you to write me a letter as to why you chose the path that you did. I kept that letter, and I had it laminated because I wanted to see what your views were after you had supposedly been rehabilitated. Please read it for me and your Nana."

I look at Uncle Scott and think to myself, it's not fair for me to have to read that letter. I wrote that my first week here when they locked me away alone in my cell and I was on suicide watch. I was angry at the world; yes, I blamed my parents. No, I didn't want to account for my actions, but that was two years ago! He looks and says, "Jackson, we're waiting," as he drums his fingernails on the table.

Fighting back tears, I begin to read.

> Stolen Opportunities
> I never had the chance
> to be all that I could be.
> Opportunities I should have had
> were stolen away from me.
> My mother was a hustler;
> my father was the same.
> I was conceived out of lust,
> so understand my pain.
> No one ever tried
> to bring out the best in me.
> If I were only shown some love,
> no telling who or what I'd be.
> My life was lived so fast;
> to me this was the norm.
> Sometimes I often wonder,
> Why was I even born?

I lower my head and can't finish any more of the poem; I hear Uncle Scott's message loud and clear.

The last things on the table are my certificates of completion, which include my GED, my anger management certificate, the accelerated reading and math class that I had taken, and my computer training certificate. Having read all of the negative headlines, I wonder if any of these achievements will even matter.

Uncle Scott sighs and says, "Jackson, I know this has been a long, hard road for you, and I am very proud of you and your progress; however, my job is pretty much done!" I start to sense abandonment, and I begin to feel a bit panicked. He continues by saying, "It's now up to you. You are the one who has to prove to that judge that you are not that same fifteen-year-old kid that we are looking at here in all of these articles." He picks the paper up off the table and holds it up close to my face with one hand. "No, you do not have to answer any of the questions that I just asked you today; but tomorrow you will! I want you to take that letter that you wrote to me over two years ago and think about it long and hard! You should be able to answer the question, how did you get here? And what you will do to make sure that you will not return?" He looks at me and says, "I believe in you, son, and if it were up to me, you would be walking out of here today."

Nana then grabs my hand and says, "Jay, you know that I love you and I will be here for you no matter what!" I somehow feel like they know something that they are afraid to tell me, almost as if they are trying to convince themselves that they believe what they are saying. I look at them both, and I feel like a total failure. Uncle Scott and Nana are all that I have left, and they are the last two people on earth whom I want to give up on me—which is what I feel is happening.

Uncle Scott notices my discomfort and says, "Jackson! Hold your head up, kid!" He then goes on to say, "If you find a path that doesn't have any obstacles, it probably doesn't go anywhere." I think about that for a second and manage to conjure up a slight smile as I give him two thumbs up. *I'm sure that I will figure out what that means soon enough,* I think.

I begin to regain my composure, and I look them both straight in the eyes and say, "I won't let you down." I then grab my things, walk back up to the front, turn around in their direction, and mouth the words "See you in the morning." The guard opens the gate and does the humiliating search again, and I then proceed toward my cell.

Directly across from my cell is the small recreation room. It has a few tables and chairs, a couple of board games, some cards, and a television. Since it is visiting day, the room is empty—except for Patches. His real name is Calvin, but he was given the nickname Patches because he is big and black with a bald head that he cuts himself with a straight razor, leaving patches all over it. Since I have been in this place, he has yet to have a visitor or receive any mail. Everyone whispers behind his back and refers to him as crazy because he never smiles, talks, or makes acquaintances with anyone—but no one is brave enough to say it to his face.

He is known for always having a book in his hand, and he rips the front cover off so no one knows what he is reading. No one ever knows what this guy is thinking, and for some strange reason, I like him.

Patches and I are in the same therapy group together. The group is made up of a diverse group of six individuals, and we meet with the counselor, Mrs. Franklin, once a month. Everyone in the group gets the chance to talk about his family, upbringing, and the circumstances that led him to be placed in confinement. I was put into therapy the first month that I entered this facility, and I must admit that in the beginning, I was uneasy about opening up. I couldn't understand how anyone would want to talk about his life just to sit back and have a bunch of strangers pass judgment. After the first few months, I started to relax, because after hearing everyone else's heartbreaking stories and tales of dysfunctional lives, it became easy; my life didn't seem so bad in comparison.

Take Jermaine, for example. He is a short, dark-skinned brother in dire need of a dentist for his massive overbite. Before he was incarcerated, he had been on his own since he was twelve years old. His mother's boyfriend didn't like him, and when the boyfriend asked the mother to choose, she chose the boyfriend. Jermaine was forced to live on the streets, and in his mind, his only means of survival was to join a street gang. He hardly ever went to school anyway, so he just dropped out and started selling drugs. He got caught while trying to sell to an undercover agent.

Then there is Debonair (that is actually his birth name, but everyone calls him D). He is a high yellow brother with curly hair. He says his mother had him when she was just fifteen years old and he met his father only once. He started running in the streets at the age of eleven because his mom was so busy having babies by different men that pretty soon she forgot about him. He left home when he was thirteen and joined a gang. He says that his mother never even noticed that he was gone. He got picked up for carjacking and breaking into houses.

The white boy of the group is Timothy. He was diagnosed with attention deficit disorder, and when he doesn't take his medication, he likes to start fights and throw things. Before he got locked up, he lived in a small suburb outside Detroit in a trailer park with his mother. He started smoking cigarettes at the age of twelve. He got arrested because he set his mother's trailer on fire when she smoked his last cigarette and she wouldn't give him any money to buy more. She managed to make it out of the house with his two brothers, but the fire spread to five other trailer homes, causing those families to be displaced.

The last person in the group is Jonathan. He is a Hispanic, preppy-looking dude whose father is a doctor. He is an only child who lived in the suburbs with both of his parents in a huge house off the lake. His parents were always vacationing in and out of town, leaving him home alone. Out of boredom, he started experimenting with different types of prescription pain pills that he found in their medicine cabinet. Jonathan claims that he likes feeling spaced out of this world; he was instantly addicted. He got arrested for stealing his father's prescription tablets and charging his friends ten bucks for whatever kinds of drugs they wanted. Before he knew it, he had practically his entire senior class addicted to pain pills. One of the kids in his class nearly overdosed on the pills, and that kid ratted him out. Jonathan nearly cost his dad his medical license, so his father pressed charges. Jonathan hasn't had any contact with his dad since he's been in this place.

Everyone has a sad story except for Patches. Well, we don't really know what his story is because he never opens up. The counselor has tried numerous times to get him to talk, but he always refuses. While others tell their stories, he never looks up from the coverless book that he always reads—that is, he didn't until I shared my story.

I talked about how my parents, Jackie and Big Man, owned an adult entertainment bar and about all the pretty women that I got to meet. (I had to spice it up a little.) I talked about all of the fine restaurants we visited, the trips to Disney, the mall, and all of the other fun things that happened in my life.

Everyone in the group was captivated, even Patches. No one could believe that he actually took his nose out of the book for the first time. It wasn't until I mentioned the bar and all of the pretty women that his interest was piqued; then he stared at me with eyes that looked so familiar, it almost felt as though I knew him from somewhere. I continued to talk about my life, and surprisingly, he continued to listen (to my stories only, from that day forward)! Everyone was so intrigued by me that they never even cared that I didn't talk about the reason I was here. I liked it that way, because I could completely block it out of my mind.

I feel that because Patches and I made some sort of mental connection in therapy class, being here alone with him inside of this TV room will give me the perfect opportunity to see if I can get him to open up. I really want to know his background, so I take my chances and decide to strike up a conversation with him, because after today, I might never have another chance.

"Hey Pa ... Calvin, are you watching this program on TV?" He doesn't look up from his book and remains silent. I assume this is a no and that he is not interested in talking. I am determined to take it a step further, so I ask the question "What are you reading?" He lets out a loud sigh and holds the book up so that I can see the pretend title. Since there is no cover on the book, I take it as a mind-your-own-business signal. Not yet feeling defeated, I respond by saying, "Hey, that's a pretty good book; I just finished it last week." He looks at me with a grin on his face and shakes his head; that lets me know that deep down inside, he does have some sort of feelings. Maybe after all these years, I am the one who never really tried to get to know him. After all, he was originally only supposed to be in this lockup for six months, but each time his release date came around, he always managed to get in some sort of trouble, and six months had ultimately turned into two years. Maybe he has nowhere to go.

Not wanting to bother him anymore, I grab the remote and change the channel. Since there is no cable in this place, our options are limited to local channels only. At four o'clock in the afternoon, the only thing on is either a talk show or one of those judge shows.

I opted for the judge show because there is a young black dude on this particular episode who looks to be about my age, and I am curious as to why he is there.

The judge wastes no time and asks this brother his name. His shoulders are slumped over, and he mumbles some words that I can hardly understand. She looks him straight in the eyes and yells so loud that my ears start ringing. "Young man, this is my courtroom, and you will respect it. Pull your pants up, straighten your head up, and speak clearly into the microphone."

Patches looks up from under the book he is reading and gives me a look as if to say "Haven't you had enough of judges?" I pay his look no mind, and as I begin to study this lost-looking kid on the television screen, the first things that I notice are his nappy hair and baggy clothes. (I can honestly say that it is like looking at the man in the mirror.) What interests me the most about this person is the lack of respect he holds for anyone. *Was that really me two years ago?* I ask myself.

He was a seventeen-year-old high school dropout who lived with his father. His mother moved away, and he had not seen her in over three years. His neighbor had accused him of breaking into her car and stealing some items while causing five hundred dollars' worth of damage to the vehicle. Although she cannot provide evidence of the crime, she tells the judge that she saw him selling some items that she believed were hers. The judge apologizes to the woman for her losses but says that she cannot make this young man pay for the items because she has no evidence of him committing this crime.

The young man begins to laugh, and the judge lets him have it all over again. This time the yelling is even louder. "By no means does this case prove your innocence. You may have gotten away with it this time, but the next time, you may not be so lucky. Your life is on a path that is headed in the wrong direction, and if you don't turn it around, you will be looking at one of two places—jail or the cemetery."

She continues by asking him what his plans for the future are. He bows his head and hunches his shoulders like a lost puppy. His response is, "I'm only seventeen; there's still time for me to figure out something. Maybe if my mom hadn't left and my dad did not work so much, I probably would have stayed in school." She looks at him and says, "That's the answer I was searching for—the reason you were not in school." It is obvious that this young man needs some direction. The judge begins to feel sorry for him; the tone in her voice becomes calm and nurturing. "Yes, young man, you are still young, but at this rate, seventeen will soon turn into twenty, twenty-two, twenty-seven—and then who will you blame."

Wow! *That cut deep,* I think to myself.

The judge's demeanor is stern. "I am sure you feel like you have been failed, but you have made it this far. Now the time has come when you have to stop blaming others and take responsibility for yourself! I wish

I had the answers as to why your mother left, or why your dad cannot really be there, but I don't! What I do know is that today is the first day of the rest of your life, and you have a choice as to what you want to do with it!"

This case is really touching me, and if I am not mistaken, I think I notice Patches paying attention as well. The judge promises the young man that she will help him get his high school diploma and some type of job training if he really wants the help. The young man finally humbles himself and agrees.

The neighbor, who is standing on the other side of the courtroom, comes across the room to give the young man a hug. She even seems happy to see him getting the help that he so desperately needs. Nana's favorite saying is "God moves in mysterious ways." This must be one of his ways, because I feel not only that that judge has just possibly saved that young man, but that she has also just saved me.

Eager to get to my cell, I immediately jump up from my chair, and as I proceed to turn the television off, an unfamiliar voice says, "Hey, bro." I look around to see who it is, and to my surprise, it is Patches. I am shocked, because this is the first time in two years that I have actually heard him speak.

"Good luck tomorrow," he says in a deep, sincere voice.

"Thanks, man," I say, still amazed that he is not a mute. I am excited, so I continue talking because I don't want the conversation to end. "Hey, maybe after I'm released tomorrow, I could write to you and send you some magazines and books?" I say, speaking positive energy into the universe (something that we learned in therapy).

He looks at me and says, "That would be nice, but I won't need them." I think about it for a second and I say, "So you will be standing in front of the judge tomorrow also, right?"

He suddenly gets an odd look on his face before he says, "Yes"; and then his face lights up right before he speaks again. "I'll most definitely be getting judged tomorrow; I will finally get to see my mom."

I look at my newfound friend, glad that he finally has something to look forward to "Well, good luck to you too, man!"

I make a mental note to say a special prayer for Patches. Maybe this time he will finally be released; I really want him to see his mom. *Wow*, I think, *God sure has been working overtime today. I hope he doesn't tire himself out; I really need him to show up bright and early with me in court tomorrow.*

—

11

Alone in my cell, I sit at the small metal table and stare at the laminated letter given to me by Uncle Scott. I silently read my own words *"Stolen Opportunities ... over and over again."*

Michael is the first person to pop into my mind, and I start feeling sad ... he is really the victim in all of this! I am the one who stole his opportunities!

So many emotions race through my mind, and I no longer blame Jackie for my troubles; she loved me the best that she knew how.

I stare at the array of photos, cards, and letters taped to my wall—all sent to me by Nana, Uncle Scott, and Grandpa Jackson—and I realize that I was given plenty of opportunities; I had somehow managed to blow them all.

Since I have been in this place, writing has become my favorite pastime.

I reach inside the small desk to grab a pen when I spot the letter and postcard sent to me from Grandpa Jackson over a year ago, when he was in Africa. I pull them both out and hold them close to my heart. The postcard is a picture of Dr. Martin Luther King Jr. with the words "The ultimate measure of a man is not where he stands in moments of comfort and convenience, but where he stands at times of challenge and controversy" On the back of the postcard it reads,

Grandson, I found this card and, absolutely loved it. I know these words may seem bigger than you right now, but someday soon, I hope that you will understand the meaning.
Love always,
Grandpa Jackson

Grandpa Jackson is my dad's (Big Man) father. He wrote to me every single week. This particular letter he apologizes for not being more involved in my life. *I could never blame him.* He also apologized for Big man; asking me to find it in my heart to forgive him. *This letter is deep.*

He closed out the letter by saying "It's not his fault grandson; I really messed up." Although I will no longer blame Big Man for my troubles; I don't believe that I can ever forgive him for his actions. This is one promise that I cannot make; since he freely walked out of my life two years ago. *Big Man no longer exists in my mind.*

Unfortunately, I never got the chance to respond to this letter. Grandpa never made it back from Africa. According to Nana, he died in a freak accident while horseback riding on that vacation. I really miss him. That's why I cherish this letter and postcard. I think that he would be proud to know that he was right—a day before my eighteenth birthday, I finally understand what the "measure of a man" means.

Desperate to clear my mind, I grab my pen and notepad and begin to jot down my thoughts. I stay up half the night writing.

I am just about finished with the letter when the bell rings, signaling us that lights are about to go out in ten minutes. I polish up the rest of the letter and tuck it inside of my jacket pocket, along with the postcard of Dr. Martin Luther King, before I kneel down to pray.

I pray for Michael and ask for forgiveness. I send out a special prayer for Patches and Jackie. I thank him for giving me my Nana and Uncle Scott, and I pray for him to give me the strength to make it through the night. I will worry about tomorrow, tomorrow.

DECISION DAY

The next morning I awake to loud sirens with the officers yelling "Code blue!" It is so hectic that I do not even get a chance to shower. An officer opens my cell and says, "Hurry up; the whole floor is on lockdown." I grab my jacket and what few belongings I can find before being hustled off to a holding cell in another part of the building. As I sit there waiting to be transported to the courthouse, I realize that the security check seems a bit more intense than usual. I ask the officer what is going on back there, and his casual response stuns me. "Some kid tried to off himself," he says like it is no big deal.

My heart feels like it wants to leap right out of my chest. I nervously ask, "Who was it?" I have a feeling that I already know the answer, but I am hoping that I am wrong.

"The weird bald-headed one," the officer says.

I feel this young man's pain, and sadness overwhelms me. "Will he be all right?"

The officer responds in an unsympathetic voice, saying, "He still had a pulse, so I think he'll pull through. We were expecting him to try something, because he's supposed to be released today; we just didn't think that it would be suicide."

I begin to reflect back on our last conversation:

"So will you be standing in front of the judge tomorrow?"

"Yes, I'll most definitely be getting judged tomorrow."

Now I know the judge that he was referring to—God.

I am puzzled as to why this young brother was so afraid of the outside world. Could things actually be that bad? If I get released, I will make it my personal business to connect with him, if it is not too late.

Before I can finish my thoughts, the officer opens the gate and handcuffs me, and I am escorted outside. It is a bitterly cold day in Detroit, with the snow falling hard and the wind blowing so strong it makes fifteen degrees feel like it is well below zero. Even though it is freezing cold, I am burning up all over on the inside because every news station is posted outside of the juvenile detention facility, all with their cameras pointed toward the van that I am getting ready to ride in. The deck is indeed stacked against me, but there is no way that I am going to give up.

The van pulls up, and an officer instructs me to step inside. When I look at his nametag, I see that it reads Officer Green—the same officer who had arrested me after the shooting. Since he is not a big fan of me, he starts to chuckle when he sees that I am struggling to enter the vehicle wearing handcuffs. He is getting a kick out of me being helpless, and he shoves my head into the van so hard that I feel it might explode. I understand some people will never forgive me. I look up at Officer Green and give him a deep and earnest smile and say, "I guess it comes with the territory." I can tell after my response that he regrets his actions. "Sorry, young man, it's just that it is cold out here; I did not mean any harm." I look up and think to myself, *God, you do get up early.*

The van stops, and Officer Green opens the door. He leads me through the garage that connects to the elevator. We take the elevator up to the floor of the juvenile court building. I break out into a cold sweat, as the floor is swarmed by the news media. There is a lot of pushing and shoving, with all of the reporters trying their best to get a close-up of me.

After several minutes, we finally enter the courtroom. I then spot the judge in her long, black robe, wearing reading glasses, carefully looking over some documents. My heart makes a thumping sound. This is not the first time I've had to face her, but I am sure hoping that it will be my last!

I glance over at Nana, who is sitting next to a scrawny dark-skinned man with long dreadlocks and clothes that are at least two sizes too big. The one thing that I know about Nana is that she does not discriminate when it comes to making friends. I figure that man is someone she paid to escort her down here for moral support. I smile at her and stand next to Uncle Scott, who grabs my hand and whispers, "Good luck, son."

As I sit here waiting for my name to be called, I am surprised when I hear the judge say, "The State of Michigan versus Calvin Lee Roberts!" Calvin's counsel stands up with a dumbfounded look on his face. Before the judge can ask where his client is, the bailiff quickly approaches the bench, waving for Patches' attorney to follow, because it is obvious that no one has informed them as to what took place a few hours earlier.

He whispers something to the judge, and the only word that I can make out is *suicide*! The judge has a shocked look on her face, and I know that Patches didn't make it. When I see the judge lower her head and make the sign of the cross over her forehead and her heart, I want to scream! At this moment, I don't know what to feel!

She then clears her throat and says, "Could the family of Calvin Lee Roberts, along with his counsel, please step into my chambers?" His counsel steps up, and the scrawny little man sitting next to Nana briefly stands up but quickly sits back down. The judge once again repeats herself: "Could the family of Calvin Lee Roberts please step into my chambers?" This time no one moves. His counsel looks at her and says, "Your Honor, he has no known family on record." The courtroom becomes silent, and the attendees bow their heads. I can hear Nana whispering the Lord's Prayer, as she often does when people die.

I think about what Patches said about his mother and wonder if she is in heaven and if that is how he planned to see her again. I bow my head, make the sign of the cross, and pray that his soul is finally at peace. *Damn!*

After about a fifteen-minute recess; the judge returns to the bench to proceed with my case. "The State of Michigan versus Jayson Lee Jackson II," she says.

Okay, God, I think, it's just me and you.

The judge says, "Mr. Jackson, could you please raise your right hand." I start to feel tense, because this is the first time that anyone has ever addressed me in such a grown-up manner. She continues to speak. "After reading over your file, I am quite impressed but not totally convinced." She peeks up through her reading glasses, exposing the doubt in her eyes. "You do understand why I addressed you as Mr. Jayson Lee Jackson II?"

I take a deep breath and say, "Yes, ma'am, I believe so."

"Can you tell me why?" she asks piercingly.

My heart begins to thump. "Well, ma'am, I believe it is because I am no longer a juvenile; I am now an adult."

"That is correct! And now that you are officially an adult, you have no more room for juvenile mistakes. Whatever you do from this day forward will have adult consequences; you can no longer hide behind your youth, because there is no youth left! Happy birthday, and welcome to the real world."

She continues to interrogate me before she asks the million-dollar question: "Mr. Jackson, if I decide to let you walk out of my courtroom a free man, how can I be sure that you will become a productive citizen in our society? How can I be sure that you will not pick up another gun and shoot someone else? How can I be sure that I won't be making the biggest mistake of my life?"

She shoots the questions at me so fast that I start feeling faint. Uncle Scott raises his hand to speak, but she cuts him off and says in a loud, firm tone, "No! Mr. Scott, I've been hearing from you for the past two years; I think it is now time for me to hear from Mr. Jackson." Uncle Scott backs down and nods his head in agreement, understanding that he can no longer protect me.

I step up to the podium, and just when I think I have it all under control, the little boy that is still left inside of me comes out, and I begin to cry. I am not trying to gain sympathy; I just can't control it. The tears flow and I can't seem to stop them. I turn to look in Nana's direction for some reassurance, but I somehow manage to lock eyes with the stranger sitting next to her instead. I can't believe it—all the weight loss in the world could never make me forget those familiar-looking eyes; they are the same as mine! That is definitely Big Man! It is such a shocker to be in the same room with the man who should have protected me instead of walking away from me. Now here he is, in court, trying to support me. After seeing him, my cries become even louder.

The judge does not seem to be fazed by my tears; I assume she sees them all of the time! She looks at me with a straight face and says, "If you are here to gain sympathy, then you had better think again; I've never been moved by tears!" I take a few deep breaths, and Uncle Scott hands me his handkerchief. As I try to get it together, she says in a very callous tone, "Are you ready now, Mr. Jackson? We can't wait for you all day!"

My confidence starts to sink, because judging by her demeanor; I believe she has already made her decision—to lock me away for a very long time!

Uncle Scott looks at me, and I can tell that he is starting to feel sorry for me, because he throws his hand up in a desperate attempt to save me. "Judge Kemp, can we please have about a thirty-minute recess? My client really needs to get himself together." He practically begs. The judge looks at her watch and says, "Okay! It's lunchtime anyway; how about we make it in an hour?" I hear Uncle Scott say "Whew" under his breath.

The judge isn't quite done; she looks at Uncle Scott and chastises him one last time. "Mr. Scott, there is a lot at stake here! I am warning you and your client that when the hour is up, we will pick right back up where we left off! If I come back into this courtroom and your client acts as though he doesn't know how he got here; that tells me there's a good chance that he will be returning!" She then stands up. "And I won't have to make my own decision. He will make it for himself! This court is now in recess." She slams her gavel down so hard on that bench that I am sure it is going to split in half.

The entire courtroom lets out a loud gasp. Before the bailiff escorts me to the small holding room, I hear a news reporter whispering into a small tape recorder, saying, "This isn't going too well for Jayson Jackson." Uncle Scott tries to follow, but I wave him off; this is no longer his fight.

The bailiff offers me lunch, but I refuse; the only thing that I need is a pen and some paper. I have a lot more reflecting to do.

Two Years Earlier

SHORTY

———

It was a little after six a.m. when I tiptoed into the kitchen. I was surprised when I found that there were three big boxes neatly stacked in front of the back door, looking like they were ready for a journey to an unknown place. Scribbled across the front in big black letters was 1234 Camp Circle Drive, Macomb, Michigan. *Whew!* I thought to myself, *I'm sure glad they weren't here last night when I slipped in two hours past my curfew! As high as I was, I know that I would have knocked them boxes over and awakened Nana, who's a light sleeper.*

Since daybreak hadn't arrived, I decided to fix myself a bowl of oatmeal instead of searching around outside in the darkness to look for my cell phone, which I had dropped the night before. I filled the tea kettle with water and put it on the stove. I reached up inside of the cabinet and grabbed a bowl, two packets of oatmeal, and some raisins. As I was waiting on the tea kettle to whistle, I couldn't help but notice that one of the boxes was labeled "scrapbooks." Once I saw that; I knew that they belonged to Jackie! *What move is she making now?* I wondered.

❊ ❊ ❊

Jackie is my mother, and she named me Jayson Lee Jackson II after my father, whom everyone calls Big Man. They were both young when they had me and got married fifteen years ago, so they were more like my brother and sister instead of my parents. Every time Jackie took me out, people would walk up to her and say, "Is that your child? You look like a baby yourself!" Jackie took this as a compliment, and from that day forward she started calling me her "Shorty" and told me that I could call her Jackie. Big Man has always been just Big Man. I liked the fact that they acted like my brother and sister, because they never chastised me or laid a hand on me; they were always too busy. The only form of discipline that they knew was to say, "Shorty, don't do that again," and that was fine by me.

Big Man made Jackie the manager of the adult entertainment bar called the Lady, which he co-owned with his father (my grandpa). Jackie gladly accepted because she knew that it was going to be the start of something big. Big Man promised her that once she learned the business, they would eventually branch out and open up their own spot.

Jackie took great pride in her job. Once she took charge, she talked Big Man and Grandpa into having the place remodeled. At first Grandpa was a little hesitant, because he was so close to retirement. "It's the best investment that you will ever make," Jackie had said while batting her eyelashes at him. He soon agreed, because he was head over heels for his daughter-in-law and he was looking forward to turning the bar over to her and Big Man so that he could travel the world. He said to her many times, "You're the best thing to ever happen to that son of mine." Jackie was flattered that Grandpa put so much trust in her, and she knew that she was going to make him very proud.

Jackie wanted to learn everything that there was to know about running a business, so she was always on the go. When she wasn't at the bar, she was in and out of town at different bar conventions or business seminars, trying to learn new and fresh ideas so that the Lady could thrive. It was proving to be a great success, because once the remodeling was done, it went from being an old watering hole to an upscale establishment.

The next thing that Jackie did was transform the female dancers. When she put her finishing touches on the girls, the business went through the roof. The Lady was then known for having some of the hottest dancers in the state of Michigan. Jackie made their costumes, did their makeup, styled their hair, and made up their routines; they loved her and paid her well. Jackie also learned how to run the bar, so when a bartender called in sick, she would step in and fix drinks. If the photographer didn't show, she took pictures; and if the cook was moving too slow, she would even fry some chicken.

The only part of the bar that Big Man would not let her near was the basement. Big Man had been running an after-hours club in that basement for years. When the bar closed at two a.m., patrons could pay twenty dollars to walk through a special door, down some steps, and into his illegal establishment. There you could shoot craps or play pool, blackjack, or poker. It was equipped with a full bar, a few slot machines, and a small dance floor. He only opened his spot up on the weekends, and he made plenty of money. Jackie didn't bother Big Man and what she called "his juke joint"; she was too busy running the Lady, and Grandpa was busy counting down the days till his retirement.

As the business started demanding more and more of Jackie's time, she had no choice but to leave me with her parents (my nana and papa) because Big Man always claimed to be just as busy. I was only one year old at the time, and Nana was happy to step in because she didn't approve of the lifestyle that Jackie and Big Man lived.

Jackie could care less how Nana felt about her and Big Man's lifestyle, and she wasn't afraid to say to her, "I know that you don't approve of how me and Big Man earn our living, but it pays the bills. This living arrangement for Shorty is only temporary; I am still his mother, and any major decisions that you decide to make will have to come through me first." She scolded Nana like she was doing her a favor instead of the other way around. Nana nodded in agreement because she didn't want to risk Jackie taking me away from her and Papa, as she had threatened many times before. Nana also knew that at the fast pace that Jackie and Big Man were moving, it would be a long time before they settled down. (Nana was right, too, because that was over fourteen years ago, and I'm still here with her.)

At that time, I didn't mind; I loved living with Nana and Papa. They gave me lots of attention, and I hardly even missed Jackie or Big Man. Papa taught me how to fish, he bought me my first baseball glove, and he would even shoot baskets with me and the next-door neighbor, Michael, who became my best friend. Nana was the greatest; she made the sweetest pancakes and delicious homemade cookies, and she gave me the biggest hugs and kisses. I loved them both.

Since Jackie and Big Man were hardly ever around, Jackie tried her best to make up for it in a big way when she did show up. When I'd see her car pull up, my eyes would light up like a tree during Christmastime because that's just what she made it feel like. She would step out of the car looking stunning, and she always had a handful of gifts—most of them for me! If she looked at my face and saw the slightest bit of sadness in it, she did everything in her power to make me smile, and a trip to

Toys"R"Us or the mall usually did the trick. I had every wrestling toy, video game system, the latest Michael Jordan shoes, polo shirts, and anything else I dreamed of. We went to Disney World and amusement parks, ate at the best restaurants, and I had parties for just about every occasion you can think of. I had so much stuff that when Michael did come over, I shared all of it with him.

The latest surprise had come a few months before, when Jackie walked into my bedroom and woke me up. She said, "Shorty, I know that your sixteenth birthday isn't for a couple of months, but I wanted to give you the first half of your gift now," and she handed me an envelope. I jumped out of bed and grabbed the envelope out of her hand. Once I had opened it, I jumped up and down, screaming, "Thank you, Jackie; this is sweet!" I was so elated that I didn't even pay attention to Jackie putting her index finger over her mouth, signaling for me to keep quiet because Nana was walking up right behind me.

"What's all the excitement about?" asked Nana

"I'm going to driver's training; I'm finally going to get my learner's permit," I said, still excited.

Nana looked grimly at Jackie and said, "J, step into the other room, please." I stepped out of the room, but I could still hear what Nana said. "Just how long do you plan on buying this child's love? Are you aware that the school sent a letter here yesterday, informing you that this boy has been suspended indefinitely? You're going to need to pay for summer school, not some driving school," Nana said in a disappointed tone.

Jackie shot back at her, saying, "I'm not buying anybody's love! That's my child, and he can have whatever he wants. As far as school is concerned, that's all been taken care of. I had a meeting with his principal the other day, and she told me that Shorty was kicked out for some missing assignments and skipping class. I told her that maybe if the teachers weren't so boring and made the curriculum more exciting, she wouldn't have to worry about him skipping class."

I heard Nana shout, "What?" because she couldn't believe what had just come out of Jackie's mouth.

Then Jackie continued telling the story. "The principal had the nerve to tell me that's it's not her problem, but mine! I told that principal that it is her problem, because she just lost a student and she's the one who's going to have to report to the school board and explain why her enrollment is declining!"

Nana said with disdain in her voice, "I can't believe you!"

I sat in the hallway laughing my butt off because Jackie didn't tell Nana the full story! She left out the part when she asked the principal to step outside. Once that poor lady did, I'm sure that the she wished that she hadn't, because Jackie became loud and belligerent! Jackie called her a liar for saying that I was a troublemaker, a bully, and part of a gang. Nana had always said that Jackie had a potty mouth because she could say some mean and nasty things. Well, her mouth was in rare form that day; she called that lady every bad name she could think of. And before the principal turned to walk away, Jackie slapped her right across the face! The lady didn't even try to defend herself. Instead, she said, "Parents like you are what ruins our youth," and she proceeded back into the building before ordering us both off of the premises before she called the police.

"That's why he needs his driver's permit," Jackie said, trying hard to make Nana see her point. "As soon as he turns sixteen in a couple of months, I'm buying him a car so he can drive himself to his new school." When Jackie said the word "car," I was even more excited; I didn't care what Nana thought, this was the best half-birthday gift ever!

Nana just didn't understand the relationship that Jackie, Big Man, and I had. Nana had agreed to step in and help raise me because she knew that Jackie and Big Man were both young and had a lot of growing up to do; she just never anticipated the irresponsible behavior they were now showcasing! That's why she let them go on about their business. Nana was hoping that someday they would be responsible enough to raise me by themselves, but she didn't foresee that happening anytime soon. Nana really hated the fact that I called them by their names. "What kind of parents would allow their child to call them by their first names? That's just foolish," she said to Jackie. However, Jackie didn't see it that way, "Well, Mother, I like being my child's friend—something that I wish you had been when I was his age!" This hurt Nana's feelings, so she just left it alone.

Jackie and Nana's relationship had been strained since before I was born, and it became common practice for Jackie to verbally attack Nana. Nana hardly ever stood up to her, and from the stories that Jackie told me, it was because Nana blamed herself for Jackie having a child and marrying young. I guess that's why she let Jackie chase whatever dream she was going after, as long as she didn't drag me into the middle of it. But now that I was getting older, Jackie was starting to have a greater influence on me, and Nana just couldn't seem to stop it.

✳ ✳ ✳

—

The tea kettle started to whistle, and I hurried to the stove to turn it off, being careful not to wake anyone. I poured the oatmeal, raisins, and hot water into the bowl and set it on the table so that it could cool. I walked over to the boxes and pushed them from in front of the door, and a big 11×14 scrapbook fell out onto the floor. I looked at the beautiful book with bright red, yellow, and orange patterns all over it and thought back on the day that Jackie and I had put that book together.

* * *

I was about ten years old at the time. Jackie came home from her fashion design class and said, "Shorty, would you like to help me with a project?" My little ten-year-old eyes lit up, because I loved being in her presence. She had scissors, tape, glue, and a gigantic box of pictures. She said, "The object of this project is to take most of these pictures and turn them into a story." She dumped all of the pictures on the floor and said, "Now, Shorty, we are only going to use the best ones."

I looked at Jackie and said, "They all are pretty, just like you"! And they were, because Jackie had never taken a bad picture in her life. She was tall with mocha-colored skin, a thin nose, chiseled cheeks, and great big dimples. Her hair was fine and wavy, so she always wore it straight back in a ponytail. She was beautiful.

This book was for her fashion design class, and she wanted it to be perfect. It was her final project, and it had to be original. Her instructor wanted her to make a scrapbook of all different types of fashions from magazines, old books, or whatever else she could find. Well, Jackie didn't need any magazines, newspapers, or books; she had enough photos to fill up hundreds of books. "Hell! I've been into fashion ever since I set foot down here on this earth, and it doesn't get any better than Jacqueline Jackson," she said as she put her hand up and slapped me a high five.

Jackie was very photogenic and loved taking pictures. She said that "there's a story behind every picture, and a picture is worth a thousand words." Although I had seen these pictures over a hundred times, each time I looked at them was like seeing them for the very first time, because each time they seemed to tell a different story.

As we both sorted through the many photos, she told me all the stories behind the pictures. She made sure that she shared every detail of her life with me (yes, even the ugly stuff). She made me promise her that I would never make the same mistakes that she had made. Her words were, "Shorty, always live your own life, and don't let anyone steal your happiness."

Jackie meant that literally, too, because when Nana put me on the basketball team and the coach took me out of the game because I fouled another player, Jackie was mad! She ran down those bleachers with her tall stiletto heels on and put her finger right in Coach's face. "You idiot! Put my Shorty back in the game; the other kid should have moved out of the way!" Nana was sitting in the crowd, holding her chest, looking like she was about to have a heart attack. Everyone on the team started laughing. Jackie walked up to me as my head was bowed down and said, "Shorty, are you ready to leave?"

I looked at her and said, "I guess so."

She grabbed my things and said, "Let's go!" She then looked at the coach and said, "My Shorty ain't a benchwarmer; he's the best player on the team." I left the bench feeling glad that she did that, because Coach seemed to favor Michael anyway. I threw up my two fingers in a peace sign to my ex-teammates and followed Jackie out the door. Nana and Coach both stood there with their mouths wide open as Jackie and I left the building. I was in the ninth grade when that happened, and I haven't cared about playing ball since.

It took us two days to finish the scrapbook project, and it turned out nice. Jackie's life was bigger than any book you could read; it was more like a miniseries. She had photos starting from the beginning of her life up until about three days before the present. She had pink dresses, white dresses, swimsuits, evening gowns, leather pants, fur coats, expensive bags, lots of gold and diamonds, and so much more!

When she turned the book in to her instructor, she got an A. The entire class was fascinated and in awe of her fabulous life. They thought that she was a celebrity, because only a celebrity could afford those types of fashions. Her instructor told her that she should probably look into doing scrapbooking to earn extra cash, because people would pay good money to have their photos turned into stories.

Jackie thought long and hard about it because she loved money. If there was any way that she could earn it without punching a clock, she at least tried it. So when her instructor told her that she could set her up with a few clients, Jackie agreed. "You can never have too many hustles, Shorty," she said to me. And she believed this, because the last time I counted, she had about five different ones.

I continued to flip through the pages until I ran across the page that read, "Happier Times 1975." It was the same family photo that Nana had hanging above the fireplace in the living room. Jackie was six months old and was wearing a pretty, ruffled baby-blue dress and a matching headband. She looked like a baby doll lying in the arms of Uncle Scott, who had on a matching blue suit and a white shirt with one of the biggest collars I had ever seen. He was a chubby five-year-old kid with pale skin and two missing front teeth. Papa, who was the patriarch of the family, stood in the back, towering over everyone. He was a tall, darker-skinned man with a big afro, neatly trimmed sideburns, and a thick mustache. Next to Papa stood Nana; she was short and petite with caramel-colored skin; thick, wavy hair that she always kept pinned up; light-brown eyes, and pearly white teeth.

When I asked Jackie why she had labeled this "Happier Times," she said, "This is probably the only time that I was happy in my childhood, because I was too young for your Nana to boss around." She went on to tell me about her childhood and what happened between her and Nana.

Jackie was Nana and Papa's only daughter. They raised her in the same house they still live in on the east side of Detroit back in the late '70s, when they migrated there from the south. Since they both had little education, Papa took a job working in the factory for Chrysler while Nana stayed at home and raised their two kids.

Nana had always dreamed of going back to school and continuing her education. She was hoping that maybe someday she would become a lawyer or a schoolteacher; but with two kids and not a whole lot of money, she knew that wasn't possible. So she did what she thought was the next best thing—live that dream through her children.

While Papa worked long twelve-hour days at the factory, Nana devoted all of her time and energy to her two kids. She sometimes watched the next-door neighbor's, Ms. Betty's, child, who ultimately became Jackie's best friend.

Nana tried to be the best mother to her children because she never had a mother herself; she was given away at birth. Nana was very active in the PTA, worked in the cafeteria, and volunteered for just about every school function there was—everyone knew who Mrs. Scott was! Uncle Scott played basketball, baseball, and football until he graduated from high school and joined the military. Once he was gone off to the military, Nana had more time to focus on Jackie. She enrolled her in ballet, beauty pageants, dance, cheerleading, gymnastics—you name it, Nana made her do it!

Jackie enjoyed these things early on because it was never about winning or losing for her, it was about having fun (at least that's what she thought it was about until Nana chastised her for not trying hard enough). When Jackie did not place first in her dance competition, Nana made her watch the videotaped performance over and over again until she felt confident that Jackie understood what she had done wrong. Nana would say, "We are striving for perfection." (Jackie thought it had been perfect, but if she had said so, it would only have made things worse) The next time there was a competition, she was ready! She stood taller, danced harder, practiced longer, smiled wider, and did whatever else it took to please Nana. However, that still didn't matter, because Nana was (unknowingly) obsessed! She continued pushing Jackie, not realizing that she was not pushing her forward but was pushing her away.

After years and years of trying to please Nana, Jackie had lost all motivation. The competitions were no longer fun for her, and she slowly started pulling away.

Their relationship changed for the worse the summer before Jackie's senior year in high school. Jackie was set to perform in a gymnastics competition where the first prize was a gold medal and a $10,000 scholarship. Nana was so nervous that one would have thought she was the performer. She desperately wanted Jackie to win this competition because, she claimed, it would open up many doors for her. Nana hired extra trainers, put her on a strict diet, and made Jackie practice roughly five hours out of the day for three months straight.

Jackie was tired and upset. She realized that she had been doing this competition stuff for so long that her teenage years were almost gone. She never had time to hang out with friends or go to the mall, the movies, or the festivals that she heard everyone bragging about when she was in school. It was then that she made up her mind. After this competition, she was going to have a nice, long talk with Nana. She didn't know how she was going to do this without hurting her feelings, but it had to be done. This was going to be her last competition, period. If Nana didn't agree to it, then she would go and explain all of it to Papa, who had no clue what was going on. He let Nana make all of the decisions; he just went along with whatever she said. Once he heard his baby girl's cries, he would have no choice but to step in.

It was the day before the competition when Nana awoke Jackie with a long list of things that had to be done before her big performance.

She had to drop off some tickets, stop by the tailor to have her final costume fitting, go and have her teeth professionally whitened at the dentist's office, and have her hair done at the mall. Nana looked at her watch and told her that they were on a tight schedule and she should be back in less than four hours. She then handed Jackie the keys to her car. She told Jackie to remember the diet that she was on and that if she stopped to get something to eat, to make sure that it was a salad. Jackie listened to Nana and all of her demands, and she suddenly started feeling resentment. Jackie was hoping and praying that she could hold on for one more day, because she knew that if Nana barked another order at her, she just might lose it. She took the keys and said, "Yes, ma'am," and trotted down the stairs.

The first stop that Jackie made was Debbie's house. She knocked on the door to see if Debbie wanted to ride with her, but Debbie wasn't there; Ms. Betty had signed her up for a college tour and she wasn't going to be able to make it to the competition. Jackie was disappointed when she handed Ms. Betty one ticket instead of two. "Are you still coming tomorrow?" asked Jackie. Ms. Betty said, "I wouldn't miss it for the world; I know how long your mother has been waiting on this!" This confirmed what Jackie already knew—this really wasn't about her. Jackie was more hurt than anyone could imagine; she had been working hard all of these years just to live out another person's dreams. She was pissed!

Jackie jumped into the car and headed to the nearest fast-food restaurant; she was going to have her nice, fat cheeseburger. She pulled into a Wendy's drive-through and ordered a double cheeseburger combo with a biggie fry and a Coke. After she sat there and stuffed herself, she headed to the mall so that she could cancel her hair appointment.

When she pulled into to the mall, there was a red convertible Mustang speeding through the parking lot. They both were racing for the same parking space, but Jackie whipped into it first. The driver of the Mustang was tailgating Jackie's car so closely that he accidentally ran into her bumper. She was furious! She jumped out of her car cursing, screaming, and causing a big scene. The driver of the Mustang got out of his car, and once he laid eyes on Jackie, his words were, "Wow you are so beautiful!" Jackie looked at the big, tall, handsome, clean-shaven man and said, "What does that have to do with anything? You tore up my damn bumper!" She continued cursing and causing a scene.

He said "Calm down; it's just a scratch. How can a young lady as beautiful as you are have such a filthy mouth?" She looked at the car and immediately became embarrassed by her actions. He reached into his pockets and pulled out a big roll of bills. He peeled off three crispy $100 bills and said, "I do apologize; here's for your troubles." She looked at the money, and her eyes grew wide, but she knew that she couldn't accept it; the scratch wasn't even that bad. His car had more damage than hers. "That's okay, sir; I can't take that, and please pardon my language. I'm just going through a lot right now." He started laughing, and Jackie started cursing all over again. "What in the hell is so funny?" Jackie screamed.

"You just called me sir! That's what's so funny," he replied.

"Well, I don't know how old you are, and I'm sure you wouldn't like me to call you boy!" Jackie snapped back.

He looked at her and said, "So you really don't know who I am?" Jackie looked closely at the man, and then she buried her face in her hands because she could not believe who was standing in front of her—her very first crush! He had once been a friend of Uncle Scott. They had played on the same football team; he had been the star quarterback. She'd had the biggest crush on him, but since he was five years older than she was, he had only seen her as Scott's little sister. She had not seen him since Uncle Scott's graduation, and she couldn't believe how much he had changed. He was much bigger than she remembered, and the reason that she didn't recognize him was that he had on a baseball cap. She still remembered his million-dollar smile and deep dimples; it was indeed Jayson Jackson! She was impressed; not only was he more handsome than she remembered, but it was also obvious that he had money.

He looked at her and said, "You really have grown up!" Jackie started blushing. He then shoved the bills in her hand, refusing to take no for an answer, along with a business card for his friend's collision shop. "Tell him Big Man sent you; he'll take care of you."

After they made a little small talk, Big Man noticed that she'd become a little more relaxed. He then decided to ask if he could see her again. "Sure," Jackie said. She remembered the extra ticket that she had to her competition and said, "How does tomorrow sound?" She slid the ticket into his hand. She really didn't think that he would come, but she wanted him to have it anyway. He gladly accepted it and told her that he was looking forward to seeing her then.

After their encounter, Jackie decided to get her hair done and teeth bleached after all; she had her eyes set on a bigger prize. Jackie finally made it home later on that evening, and Nana was upset because she had been gone all day. Jackie didn't care; she ignored Nana and headed straight up to her room on cloud nine.

On the day of the competition, Jackie awoke to a big surprise—Uncle Scott had taken leave and flown in for what he believed to be Jackie's biggest day. She was ecstatic because she had not seen him in over a year. The house was filled with roses. Uncle Scott bought her a dozen, Papa bought her a dozen, and a delivery man pulled up to the house with another two dozen. Nana accepted the package and took it upon herself to open up the card that was attached.

When Jackie finally made it down the stairs, she saw Nana reading her card, and at that moment she had had enough. Jackie looked at Nana and said, "I despise you, and I'm sick of trying to live out your dream! You have made my life a living hell, and it all ends today!"

Nana was taken aback by all of this and didn't understand. Her voice started cracking as she asked, "What has gotten into you? I thought that this is what you wanted!"

Jackie said, "I never did this for me; it was always for you! And no matter how hard I try, you are never going to be satisfied, so after this competition, I quit! If you want a damn title, then you go out there and get it yourself!" She stormed off, leaving Nana standing there stunned.

Jackie went on with the competition, and she didn't place first or second or third; she flat-out lost! For the first time since she had been competing, she felt no pressure, and that alone made her feel like she had won. Papa, Uncle Scott, and Ms. Betty all hugged Jackie and told her that she had done great. Nana didn't say a word; she was still hurt. Jackie thanked everyone and ran off to the locker room so that she could get dressed.

She changed from her costume into a pair of leggings, a fitted t-shirt, and her ballerina slippers. When she walked out of the locker room, there stood Big Man. He couldn't stop staring at her; he was mesmerized by her beauty and perfect form. Jackie was fascinated by the fact that this older gentleman was actually interested in her.

He walked up to her and handed her another dozen roses. "You were spectacular! I wanted to approach you earlier when you were with your family, but I know that they would probably try to have me arrested since I'm a little older than you!"

Jackie took the roses and then responded by saying, "Thank you! These are so beautiful, just like the roses that you sent me earlier. Now don't go worrying about my family; you leave that up to me! And besides, I'm seventeen, and I make my own rules!" Jackie then blew him a kiss and said, "I will see you tomorrow afternoon—same place where we met."

Jackie really didn't make her own rules, but she knew how to sneak and keep a secret, and during the entire ride home, she was cooking up a plan.

Later that evening, after the competition, Jackie went to Nana and Papa and told them both to have a seat. Once everyone was comfortable, Jackie's plan went into action. She looked at them both and said, "Look, I've been dancing and competing all of my life, and today, I want to put that part of my life behind me!" She looked squarely at her mother as if daring her to intervene.

Papa looked at Jackie and said, "Princess, just because you didn't win in that particular competition doesn't mean that you have to give up."

She cocked her head to the side and placed one hand on her hip and said, "Now, Dad, you know that you didn't raise a quitter! I will be a senior in high school in a few weeks, and it's time that I started thinking about my future and what direction my life is headed in."

He cleared his throat and said, "I thought that you and your mother had all of that worked out; she said that you were either going to—"

Nana quickly intervened because she remembered the conversation that she and Jackie had had earlier and she didn't want to start any more trouble. She looked at Papa and said, "No, dear, those were just prospects; the final decision is up to her!"

Jackie looked at Nana and smiled. Papa had always been nonconfrontational, and true to form, he said "Oh! So what is it that you really want to do?" *Finally!* Jackie thought. *I have them both on the same page!*

"Well I've been over there talking to Debbie, and since she will be heading off to college in a few weeks, she said that she could hook me up with her old job at the mall." Papa raised his eyebrows and said, "The mall? You know that you don't have to get a job!"

Jackie cut him off before he could finish. "This is something that I want to do! When I graduate, I just might want to be a fashion designer or a buyer at a store," she said as she pranced around and did her runway walk to soften the mood.

When they both didn't give her the feedback that she had expected, she started pouring it on thick. "And who knows, I really enjoyed the criminal justice class that I took my junior year of high school; maybe I'll go to law school like my big brother." Papa had the biggest grin on his face. *Bingo!* Jackie thought to herself. *It worked!*

Papa started getting excited, as though Jackie had already enrolled in the classes. "Wow! Now that's the talk I'm trying to hear; we will have two lawyers in the family!" Jackie felt so bad lying to Papa, but after everything that Nana had put her through, she was just hoping that she would make it to her high school graduation in one piece!

Nana was starting to lighten up when she heard Jackie say that she wanted to be a lawyer, but her joy was cut short when she said, "That's wonderful; I always dreamed of someday being a lawyer. Maybe I can help you pick out a school and we ca—"

Jackie quickly cut her off. "No!" She didn't mean for it to come out so harsh, but it was too late; the damage was done. "I need to do this alone; it's time that you two let my hand go!"

Nana had always said, "Fight for what you believe in!" And that's just what Jackie was doing—fighting to be with Big Man.

Papa looked at his wife and said, "Well, this child has a point; we can't hold on to her forever!"

The room was silent for a minute until Nana said, "What day do you start?"

Jackie turned around and lightly pumped her fist so that they wouldn't see her as she said, "Tomorrow afternoon," all the while thinking, *Maybe I should really go into sales, because I just sold to my first customers!*

✳ ✳ ✳

The next day, as promised, Jackie met Big Man at the mall. She parked Nana's car there every afternoon before she jumped into the car with Big Man. They spent the first few days getting to know each other. Big Man said to Jackie, "I want to know everything about Ms. Jacqueline Scott, Jeff Scott's little sister."

Jackie looked at him and said in a very seductive voice, "There's nothing little about me."

He started smiling as he licked his lips and said, "I like bad girls!"

Jackie really wasn't a bad girl; she just knew what she liked, and she wasn't afraid to go after it. "Well, what you see is what you get," she said. "I've been competing since before I could even write my name. I live with my parents, my brother is off in the military, I'm seventeen, I will be a senior in a couple of weeks, I've been voted most popular girl in school every year since I've been there, and I have no idea what I want to do after I graduate! And since I don't have a biological sister, Debbie is the closest thing that I have to one, and she also happens to be my neighbor. I tell her everything." (Jackie made sure she slipped in the part about Debbie in case Big Man tried some funny stuff; he would know that her whereabouts were not unknown). "I've been kind of down lately because she's going off to college in a few weeks, and I'm going to need someone to fill that void; would you be up for the challenge?" She said these words in a real take-charge kind of way.

Big Man said, "Wow! I like your style, and I love a challenge."

Jackie blushed as he grabbed her hand. "So what's your story?" she asked.

Big Man told her how he was an only child. He had been raised by his father, who worked at the factory. His mother had walked out on them both when he was about three years old. She left for a man who had more money than his father. *At least that's what he was told.* He hasn't seen her since. "Case closed, end of story" he said to Jackie pretending that he wasn't bothered by her absence. "I don't want anyone who doesn't want me; besides, I think that my pops did a great job. We hit a few rough patches, with him being a single father and all, but he had lots of help from all the females that he worked at the factory with. Everyone wanted to take care of James Jackson's son, Little Jayson, hoping that my father would marry them, but it never happened!"

Big Man's father never trusted a woman again. Money was all that he cared about and he was determined to strike it rich! He purchased a few run-down houses and a small apartment building on the east side of Detroit, fixed them up, and now he had renters—tons of them.

His father was now a wealthy man who gave Big Man whatever he wanted. He also taught Big Man that nothing was more important than money. *A seed that his father would later regret he planted.*

"It must be nice!" Jackie said. Her eyes were wide and she was totally impressed. "So tell me, how does it feel to be twenty-two years old and never have to work?"

He laughed. "You're funny. I wouldn't know how that feels, since I do have to work! My father's preparing for his retirement, so he's made me co-owner of the bar that he owns. He seems to think that I am not mature enough to run the business all by myself, so he's training me. Once he retires, I will be the sole proprietor."

"Oh, wow!" Jackie said. "So what kind of bar is it? What type of music do they play?"

Big Man hesitated; he hesitated to tell her what type of bar it was, for fear of her taking it the wrong way like most women did. He knew that he wouldn't be able to keep it from her, so he reluctantly said, "It's an adult entertainment bar.

Jackie's eyes grew even wider; that caught her off guard. "Isn't that just a dressy title for women who prance around half naked just for people to throw money at them?" she asked as she clutched her purse, ready to end the date. Big Man noticed her discomfort, and he knew what she was thinking. He was used to women feeling uncomfortable and insecure with their establishment. He looked her in the eyes and said, "Never in a million years would I let my queen take off her clothes for anybody but me," and he kissed her softly on the lips.

Jackie had a tingling sensation all over her body, and she felt like a childish little girl as she giggled when he referred to her as his queen. Jackie had never been in love with anyone before, but if this funny feeling inside of her stomach was what love felt like, she didn't want it to end! Big Man was starting to fall hard for Jackie. *Something that his father told him never to do.... fall for a woman.* He liked her beauty and her presence and loved her innocence. He could tell from the way that he grabbed her hand and kissed her lips that she was fragile and not damaged goods like the other women he had been with. He was going to make her his queen, and he promised himself that he would handle her with care.

Over the next few days, they went shopping. Big Man said, "since you're now my queen, it's time to make you look like one!" He took her on a shopping spree at Somerset Mall, one of the priciest malls outside the city of Detroit. He picked out all of her clothes, and he made sure that everything fit her body perfectly. If something was a little off, he had it tailored. He bought her expensive purses, sunglasses, shoes, and whatever else she liked. Jackie always had style and flair, but Big Man took her style to a whole new level. She had never heard of most of the designers that he picked out, and she couldn't even pronounce some of their names.

She especially liked how all of the saleswomen called him by his first name and treated him like he was royalty. She even considered it a compliment when a few of them rolled their eyes at her. Jackie had graduated from the minor leagues to the majors, and she could get used to this! She never even thought about the fact that she was moving away from one form of control with Nana into another form of control with Big Man.

That summer turned out to be the best summer of Jackie's life. Nana and Papa eased up on her, since they thought that she had a job working at the mall. They really believed that their little girl she was actually turning into a responsible adult, so they never questioned her whereabouts, as long as she was home before her midnight curfew—and Big Man always made sure that she was.

❅ ❅ ❅

It was nearing seven a.m. when the sun started beaming through the window. I closed the book on Jackie's elaborate life and placed it back on top of the box. I opened the back door and traced my steps from the back porch out into the driveway, where Jackie's brand-new Jeep Grand Cherokee sat, in hopes of finding my cell phone. I hit the power lock and thoroughly searched the truck, but the only thing that I found was my lighter; the phone was nowhere in sight. *Damn!* I thought. This was the third phone that I had lost this month, and Jackie had sworn that she wasn't going to replace another one.

I was pissed off when I walked back into the house. I put my oatmeal in the microwave for a few seconds, and just after I sat down at the table, contemplating what I was going to tell Jackie about my cell phone, I heard someone coming down the stairs.

Just as I was about to shove the first spoonful into my mouth, Nana yelled my name like the house was on fire! "Jaaaaaaay!" she screamed.

Dang! I thought. I was hoping that was Jackie! Nana probably has a laundry list of things for me to do since I am not in school this week!

"Get in here now!" she said as Detroit Channel 7 Action News music played in the background.

"So many young lives lost or ruined so senselessly," I heard her say in a repulsed tone. I automatically knew what this meant: something bad or tragic had happened, and it was on the news. There was no way around this one; I was in for another one of her long lectures. So finishing this oatmeal was a no-brainer, because once she got started, there was no telling when she would end!

"Jayson Lee Jackson II," she yelled, more adamantly than before. "Do you hear me? Come here now; you really need to see this!"

I quickly arose from the table and said, "Just a sec," as I reached inside my back pocket for my hair pick. *Oh, boy! It's worse than I thought; she called me by my birth name; a name that she swore she'd never call me.*

❅ ❅ ❅
—

It was no secret that Nana didn't like Big Man; she only tolerated him. And the fact that Jackie named me after him only added fuel to the fire, because Nana claimed that he was no good. "If you don't want your child to be just like the first, then you have no business naming him the second!" she said, chastising Jackie. Jackie didn't care. She was crazily in love with Big Man, and telling her to not to name her firstborn after the man that she loved was like telling a fish to swim without water.

Nana had never gotten over the fact that her only daughter, whose future had once been so promising, had lied to and manipulated her and Papa! Jackie kept her and Big Man's relationship a secret for over a year. Nana and Papa had no clue because Jackie was keeping her grades up, coming home before her curfew, and pretending to hold down a part-time job. They couldn't have been more proud! Then, all of a sudden, everything came to a screeching halt when Jackie was accepted to Michigan State University on an academic scholarship. Nana and Papa were so excited because their little girl was finally going to work toward fulfilling her dream of becoming a lawyer. Sadly, their world was rocked two weeks before high school graduation. Nana took Jackie to the doctor to have her physical done, and that's when the doctor broke the news: there would be no Michigan State or scholarship. Instead, there would be a baby; Jackie was pregnant!

Nana cried, and Jackie was elated. Jackie wanted to have Big Man's baby so she could get out from under Nana's roof. Big Man wanted her to have the baby so his dad would deem him responsible and turn the business over to him (which eventually worked).

Nana said that both Jackie and Big Man had their own agendas as to why they wanted to have a child, and in her eyes, neither one of their agendas was for the right reasons. I could never seem to make it to the top of their priority list.

When Nana would voice her concerns to Jackie, the only response she would get was, "Get over it, Mama; that was years ago." Nana never could get past it; she said the best thing that came from their union was me.

Nana couldn't believe how naive Jackie was. Ever since Big Man's father had retired and turned the bar over to him and Jackie, Big Man took on a whole new persona of arrogance and selfishness. Nana witnessed Jackie busting her tail to make that bar a success, only to watch Big Man take all of the credit. Nana never forgot the time that he did that interview for a new magazine called *Up and Coming Detroit,* and he never mentioned the fact that he had a wife and child. He graced the cover of the magazine, standing alone in front of the Lady looking like he was some sort of king: he was wearing an expensive suit, a full-length mink coat with matching hat, and some black alligator cowboy boots. The entire interview was about young black entrepreneurs. He was voted number one. They praised him for keeping his upscale establishment in the city and continuing to give back to the community. The article was two pages long and they quoted him as saying, "I owe everything to my dad, who afforded me this opportunity; once he hiked me the ball, I took off running!" He even bragged about the fact that he was in the process of finalizing the plans to open up a new adult entertainment venue; it was going to be bigger and better. "When people step into the building, they are going to feel like they're in Las Vegas." He concluded the article with the words "The Lady too is coming soon!"

Judging by the interview, one would have thought that he built that empire alone! Jackie didn't seem to be bothered by the article at all; she was actually excited. When Nana finished reading the article, she was floored. "Jackie, sweetie, where's your picture? Doesn't he know that there is no *I* in *team*?" she said very calmly. Jackie, always quick to defend Big Man, looked at Nana. "Oh, Mother, only you would be so worried about something as minor as that! Big Man is the one who likes to shine in front of the cameras; I like living my life behind the scenes." She held her left hand up, sporting her three-carat diamond bling. "This is all the shine that I need, at least for now!" she said with a smirk.

Nana had no idea what Jackie meant by her last statement, but she did know that "in order to be old and wise, you first have to be young and foolish." So she left it alone. She wrote it off as Jackie going through her young and foolish stage.

I put my bowl in the sink and slowly walked into the living room before Nana called my name again. When I entered the living room, she was sitting in Papa's La-Z-Boy chair—the same chair that he had died in five years earlier of a sudden heart attack. I believe that chair gave her some sort of comfort, because no one was allowed to sit in it but her.

As I quietly stood behind her, I envisioned Papa sitting there, flicking the remote control in one hand and holding a cold beer in the other, and patting the chair for me to sit down next to him. "Jayson, I'm going to explain something called the birds and the bees," he would say through slurred speech. "He would talk my ten-year-old ears off, and although I couldn't figure out what the heck the birds and the bees were, I was always fascinated by his stories! Nana would always yell for him to leave me alone and come to bed. He would respond by saying, "I'm not sleepy; I will sleep when I am dead."

So when Nana awoke one morning, and he was still sitting in that chair with his eyes closed. She knew he was dead, because he never closed his eyes in that chair. I really miss that old man, and I would have given anything to hear one of his captivating stories now instead of the drilling I was about to receive from Nana.

She was just about to scream my name again when I said; "Here I am," trying to straighten out my hair.

She turned around and said, "Boy, don't be sneaking up on me like that!

Didn't she just call me like a hundred times? I thought.

"And how many times do I have to tell you to cut your hair?" She said this like she was about to get a pair of scissors and cut it herself.

I told the first lie that I could think of, because I liked my nappy hair. "Seems as though my barber, Tone, went to Florida for Spring Break; he won't be back until next week."

"Well you better find another one before then, because you look like a criminal. Why would you want to walk around and have someone judge you before you even open your mouth?" Nana always had to take things to the extreme. Me and my boys liked to stand out; it wasn't our problem if people were afraid.

That's when she pointed to the screen; there was breaking news on. Three young African American males had unsuccessfully tried to rob a gas station. One had been shot in the leg, one was being hauled away in handcuffs, and a third suspect had gotten away on foot. "Are those the same young men whom you have been hanging around with?" Before I could even answer, Nana shot me a wicked look with those big brown eyes and said, "Don't lie to me!"

I felt like I was having an out-of-body experience as I stared at the screen. My knees locked, my arms locked, and my eyeballs bulged out of my face! It was my boys Max and Marcus, and judging from the video, they looked as guilty as sin, and their nappy hair was standing up all over the place. I nearly stopped breathing when the picture of the gas station that we had been at last night flashed across the screen. I started shaking. Who would have thought that a simple run to the gas station last night would have had this type of outcome? I had no idea as to what happened in that gas station. When I had heard sirens, I did what we always did in the city of Detroit (gunfire *or sirens; you don't look back, and run like hell!*) I had run back to the car, and I assumed that they ran home, since the gas station was right around the corner from their house. I can't believe that they were the ones who caused all the commotion. When I had made it inside the house, I couldn't call to make sure that they were okay, because I had dropped my cell phone. I hoped to God I wasn't the one they thought had gotten away!

Nana started yelling my name again. "Jay … Jay … Jay!"

I snapped out of the bad dream that I was having; only to realize that it wasn't a dream. "Huh?" I answered with a shaky voice.

"Why do you look like you just saw a ghost? Do you know those thugs?"

"No, Nana," I said with a bit of a whine, "I was just looking at their hair, and I was thinking maybe I should go and get my hair cut after all! I will probably have them shave it all off!" I was thinking this would be a good way to change my appearance in case the cops came knocking.

"I know that sometimes my eyes may deceive me, but that sure does look like that lil yellow boy that stopped by here the other day!" Nana said with uncertainty in her voice.

I took tiny breaths to calm myself before I spoke. "I can't tell; the picture looks fuzzy, and I don't think that they would do something stupid like that!" I tried to sound as persuasive as possible, because I knew that if I didn't, I would be sitting there until the following week.

"I sure hope not, either," she said, not wanting to think that I would have friends who could do something like that. "*See* how people can make one stupid mistake and ruin there their whole life?"

I'd heard her lecture many times, but each time she preached it, I acted as though it were the first. "Yes, Ma'am, I'm aware," I said, thinking this would bring the discussion to a quick close.

"Well, I just want you to know that I know you have been coming in this house way past your curfew and that you have also been sneaking out in the middle of the night. I don't know what you are up to, but I don't like it."

"No I have—"

"Don't even try it! I may have been born at night, but it sure as heck wasn't last night." Although Nana was in her sixties, she had a very sharp mind, and I sure couldn't fool her easily. "I know you were not here last night, because Michael came by to share his good news with you; it seems as though he has gotten himself a full four-year basketball scholarship to Michigan State University."

Michael had been my best friend since I was in preschool and he was in first grade, and he had been a straight-A student since I could remember. Although we hung out together, we were as different as night and day; Michael liked to chase a basketball, and I liked to chase the girls. Michael excelled in school and sports and music; and the only thing important to me was the girls, my homeboys, and a good time! We both shared similar backgrounds; his grandmother, Ms. Betty, raised him just as Nana was raising me. When Jackie took off with Big Man, his mother took off for the streets, and now Ms. Betty's hard work seemed to be paying off, while Nana's hard work and lectures seemed to go unnoticed.

"I told him congratulations and that you were up in your room," said Nana. "He went upstairs and came right back down claiming that you were asleep and that he didn't want to wake you; said he would come back today."

Leave it to Michael to get me busted, I thought. He never was a good liar; in fact, that's probably the only thing he's not good at!

"Well I knew better," she said, "so I went straight upstairs to your room and knocked on that door, and when you didn't answer, I went in, and you were nowhere to be found."

I could not believe that she had actually entered my room without me being there. The one thing that she always stood on was one's space and privacy. She believed everyone deserved their own space, and she did not believe in invading other people's privacy. Now, don't get me wrong; if she felt like something was going on, she would act—like the time Kelly's mom told Nana that Kelly had been skipping school and she thought that she may have been hiding in my room. Nana turned that room upside down with me present, pulling out all of the drawers, looking in the closet, and searching under the bed, only to come up empty-handed. Since that day she had promised to trust me and always give me the benefit of the doubt, so her unannounced entry into my room meant that we had another trust issue going on.

"Well, this time, young man, I didn't come up empty-handed! I found these here cigarettes and this thing that looks like a cigar—but I know better!" My heart nearly stopped beating. I had looked all over for those the night before, and I couldn't find them anywhere; now here they were, staring me in my face. "Nana, those are not mine" was the only thing that I could say before she cut me off.

—

41

"Well, whose are they—mine, I suppose?" she said in a very sarcastic tone. One thing about Nana was that if she knew you were being dishonest, she would never let you continue to lie, she would just preach until you were blue in the face. So I politely slid down on the sofa and prepared myself for what seemed would be a long day, and I gave her my undivided attention like the obedient child she once knew.

"Jay, you know that I won't tolerate drugs in my house. Ever since you turned fifteen, it seems as if I don't even know who you are anymore. You have been kicked out of school, staying out late, and now you want to add drugs and cigarettes to the equation?" She was acting as though I was some sort of addict who needed rehab. "I am getting up there in age, and I am not trying to bury you or come visit you behind bars, so you leave me with no other choice but to send you to California to live with your uncle Scott." I bowed my head because Nana had warned me that if she had any more trouble out of me, I would be on the first thing smoking to California! And she wouldn't let Jackie or Big Man stand in her way.

"Are you serious?" I protested.

✳ ✳ ✳

Uncle Jeffery Scott joined the army right after high school. After losing a lot of his friends to gun violence and drugs, He believed that "if you're going to live in a war zone, you might as well get an education and a little pay out of it!" And that's just what he did; he fought in Desert Storm, got a law degree, and got a beautiful Asian wife to top it all off! Uncle Scott had been all over the world to places like Japan, Germany and China. You name it, and he probably has seen it. He is now a retired colonel and a big-time lawyer on the West Coast.

When I was younger, I would spend my summer vacations with him, his wife, and his two sons. Although I did enjoy seeing many parts of the world, I did not enjoy his military ways. His two sons—Jeff Jr. and Jake—and I had to wake up every morning before the crack of dawn. "The early bird catches the worm," he would say. We had to do physical exercises, clean our rooms, and make our beds so tight you could bounce a quarter off of them. He would often say, "I'm going to make a man out of you boys!" Heck, we were only about eleven years old at the time; we could care less about being a man at that age. Those were some of the longest summers of my life. I remember him saying to me, "Private

Jackson (he called everyone by his or her last name), one day you will appreciate all of this." Well, it has been two years since my last visit, and I still don't appreciate all that hard work.

When I would call home and try to complain to Jackie, she would say, "Now, Shorty, you know boys aren't supposed to cry." There was no way I was going to move out to California with him.

✳ ✳ ✳

"But Nana, I told you those things are not mine," I said like my life depended on it.

Just as I was about to try to plead my case, a voice from the top of the stairs said, "He's right, Mom, they are not his; they're mine."

I did a double take. Did Jackie just say what I thought she had said? Now how cool is that? This will certainly earn her a star in the coolest parents hall of fame!

Although Jackie and Big Man had their own place, Jackie still occupied a room here with me and Nana. For the past couple of months, she'd been spending a lot of time here, and she'd been acting very strange; her behavior was somewhat erratic.

"What the hell do you mean they're yours?" Nana said with fury in her voice. This was my first time ever hearing Nana curse. She was mad!

Jackie stood at the top of the stairs with one hand on her hip, looking like one of the many exotic female dancers she managed. She appeared to have lost some weight, because she looked exactly like she had in the pictures fifteen years ago—skinny! She had on a fitted body suit with a long black wig that came down to the center of her back, accented with a brown-and-gold designer scarf tied around her head. Her oversized purse flung over her arm and her thigh-high boots made her look like she was on her way to a fashion photo shoot; she looked like an African goddess. She was undeniably beautiful, and she knew it!

She stormed down the stairs like she owned the place; one would have thought that Nana was the one living rent free instead of her. With a bold and fierce attitude, she stepped up to Nana and repeated herself. "I said they are my cigarettes; I must have left them in his room last night when I went to tuck him in." She smirked and winked in my direction. She might have been better off holding her tongue, though, because by the way that Nana was looking at her, it sure seemed that she would be swallowing it!

Nana started fanning herself, which meant that her blood pressure was beginning to rise. She was calm as she asked Jackie the next question. "How do you explain your car being gone if you tucked him in?"

Busted! went through my mind, but Jackie was always one step ahead; it was as if she had this whole thing rehearsed. "I let him make a quick run for me; he was back by ten!" This was truly unbelievable.

That's when Nana lost it all over again. Forget about making Jackie swallow her tongue; Nana was ready to snatch it out!

These two women were the same height, but Jackie's four-inch heels made her appear to be taller. That still didn't seem to make Nana back down, though. She screamed at the top of her lungs, "Have you lost your darn mind! This child only has a learner's permit, not a driver's license! And you know that I don't allow drugs in my house."

I still couldn't believe that Jackie had actually told that lie, but there was no turning back now; the battle had just begun. I felt I needed some popcorn, because this was about to become one heck of a show.

"What in the world were you thinking sending him out that late at night? If he had gotten stopped by the police, we all would have been in a world of trouble. Sometimes I don't know who the parent is—him or you!"

"Stop overreacting, Mom; he wasn't even gone that long, and I don't think the police will bust up this place for a measly marijuana cigarette." Jackie sure was good, because she kept the lies rolling. "I needed him to stop by the bar and pick up something for me; he put my keys back on my dresser before midnight," she snapped as she headed toward the door, leaving Nana standing there speechless! "And another thing," Jackie said with one hand on her hip, pointing at Nana as if she were scolding her, "I am still his mother, and he's not moving anywhere!"

That was the final blow, because from out of nowhere, *smack!* Nana had done the unthinkable and slapped Jackie right across the face! Jackie grabbed her face in disbelief and shock because she never saw that one coming. I guess Nana had finally had enough of Jackie's nonsense.

Nana then looked up at her with smoke practically coming out of her ears and tears rolling down her face as she said, "All of the hard work I have put into this child will not be thrown down the drain because of the bad decisions that you and his so-called father make! Jay needs friends on the playground, he needs friends at school, and in you and his father he needs role models—you know, the kind that they call parents. In other words, you two need to grow up!" It was as if Nana were a boxer, because she had definitely hit below the belt on that one.

Jackie wasn't bothered by that at all; she came back with the final swing. "That's what last night was all about, Mother," she said, rolling her head, "these!" She dangled a pair of keys in the air. "I don't appreciate what you and my so-called big brother is doing; trying to turn my Shorty against me and Big Man. Well, for the first time ever, I have to admit you are right!" Jackie said in a sarcastic voice. "It is time for me and Big Man to step up! I'm now a grown thirty-three-year-old woman who is tired of living under your roof and playing by your rules, so Shorty and I will be moving out! Big Man has bought us a condo in Macomb County."

Nana looked as stunned as ever! She never in a million years thought that Jackie would take me away from her, although she had threatened to many times before. This time it seemed that she would make good on her promise, because she had actually had a set of keys.

Nana got ready to open her mouth, determined to have the last word, but Jackie threw her hand up, making it clear that this discussion was closed. With that having been said, Nana bowed her head in defeat. The one thing that Nana knew was that Jackie was a risk taker—no testing the waters; she liked to dive in headfirst.

I was scared and excited at the same time. I had been with Nana since I was one year old, and me living with Jackie and Big Man would be like living on my own.

"Shorty, I need you to go upstairs and start packing up your things; the movers will be here tomorrow, and I want you to be packed and ready to roll," she said as if she were coming to pick me up from a two-week visit at grandma's house. I turned around to head up the stairs and caught a glimpse of Nana staring at the television screen as Channel 7 Action News was ending. I was just getting ready to go over to her and offer her a hug when there was a loud banging at the door. *Bam! Bam! Bam!* "Detroit Police; open up!"

At that moment, I almost peed in my pants. I was just about to fall to my knees and scream, "Nana, please don't let them take me; I will go to school every day, and I will even go to church on Sunday!" I started hyperventilating, and before a sound could come out, Jackie said, "Shorty! Quick! Go upstairs to my room, look under the bed, and throw that black bag with the gold lock on it out the window!"

Nana and I both looked at her and said "Huh?" at the same time.

"Just do it now!" she screamed more aggressively. Trying to get my heart rate to slow down, I moved slowly up the stairs, still in shock that the cops were actually at our door.

When I finally made it up the stairs; which seemed to take forever, I noticed that Jackie had left her cell phone on the bed, and it was ringing. Since she had just sprung the news on Nana about us moving to Macomb, I figured that it had to be Big Man calling. I normally would never answer her phone, but at this moment my, fear forced me to click the button and say, "Hello!"

A shocked Big Man said in a deep, heavy, powerful tone, "Who the hell is this?"

Shocked, but not surprised that he didn't recognize his own son's voice, I responded with a cracking voice, saying, "It's me—Shorty!" Although Big Man was my father and I longed for his affection, we did not have that father/son bond thing going on like I so desperately wanted. He was strictly a provider—nothing more, nothing less—but if there was ever a problem, he always knew how to fix it or knew somebody who could, and that's what I admired most about him.

"Damn, Shorty," his voice carried loudly through the phone. "What's going on with you, Lil man?" he asked as if he was unaware that I was now six foot two. "The police are here, and now I may be going … I mean, Jackie may be going to jail."

"What?" was all he could say before he started barking orders at me. "Now listen to me, Shorty; don't tell them anything! Don't even mention my name!"

What is that supposed to mean? I thought. I felt like I was in one of those gangster movies; what the heck was I going to tell? I sure as heck wasn't telling on myself! "Okay, I understand," I said, whispering into the telephone. When he heard me whisper, he said in an aggravated tone, "Come on, man, don't get soft on me now; you have Jackson blood running through your veins!"

So I put a little bass in my voice and said "I got it!"

"Now don't worry about a thing, Shorty. I will send my attorney down to the police station, and everything will be all right."

After I closed the cell phone, I looked under the bed and grabbed Jackie's bag with the gold lock on it. I was just getting ready to throw it over the balcony into the backyard when I noticed that the lock was not secure. I started to lock it, but my curiosity got the best of me and I decided to take a peek inside.

When I saw what was inside of the bag, I felt like I had opened up Pandora's box. *What the hell are they into?* I thought. I lifted one of the ten or more packets out and put it up to my nose, and as sure as my name is Jayson Lee Jackson II, it was some of the best-smelling weed I had ever seen. I caught a buzz just by sniffing inside of the bag. I know that I shouldn't have, but I just couldn't resist. I slipped about three of those packs into my pocket, thinking, *Jackie will never miss this!* There were stacks of $100 bills—there had to be at least $200,000 in the bag—along with several bottles of pills and several large yellow envelopes. That definitely confirmed it for me; there was no way that those cops were here for me!

MICHAEL

I was lying sprawled across Grandma Betty's long black couch when the fresh smell of roasted coffee caused me to open my eyes. I forced myself into an upright position, being careful not to aggravate the ankle that I sprained last night when I tripped over my mother, Debbie, who was passed out drunk in the middle of the floor.

I knew that it had to be well after 7 a.m., since that's the time that Grandma's coffee pot was set to brew. Coach told me that I needed to be packed and ready for basketball camp by 8 a.m., but with this throbbing ankle, that didn't seem possible.

I thought about last night and realized that my sprained ankle was a small price to pay for the valuable lessons that I learned, and I couldn't help but reflect back.

What had started out as what was supposed to be an innocent night of fun turned out to be everything but that. I left here last night with Jay in hopes of celebrating my scholarship to Michigan State University, only to end up running two miles home from one of the roughest neighborhoods on the east side of Detroit.

Running had always been very therapeutic for me, but last night when I found myself jumping over broken glass, dirty drug needles, garbage, and debris, it was no longer healing—it was all about survival.

I could still hear Jay yelling my name, but it quickly faded into an echo since I was three blocks ahead of him and his thuggish friends. As I continued to sprint through the blighted neighborhood, I spotted what looked to be three drug addicts, all gathered on one corner, looking for that two-minute rush that most likely stole all of their dreams and aspirations. I paused to say a silent prayer, asking God to please save their souls and remove them from that dangerous street corner.

My prayers were immediately answered when a police car passed by and they took off running. I slowed my run down to a jog as the police car turned around and shined a bright light in my face. "What's the hurry?" the officer said arrogantly as he exited his police cruiser.

I stopped and stood at attention—something that I had learned in ROTC (Reserve Officer Training Corps) class back in tenth grade. "Trying to make curfew, officer," I said in a very polite tone, giving him no reason to harass me.

"Well, it's after ten, and usually when I see a man over six feet running through this neighborhood, it can mean only mean one thing—trouble."

I stood there in silence, being careful not to interrupt him. The lone officer looked me over for a few more seconds before saying, "When I circle back around, I hope to see you gone!"

"You will, sir," I said, continuing to be polite. I removed my baseball cap just as he was about to pull off, and he shined the light in my face again.

"Heeeeeeey, aren't you that kid Michael Stephens, Eastside High School's power forward?" he asked, excited like he had just won the lottery. "You were Mr. Basketball last year, and you averaged twenty-eight points, fifteen rebounds, and seven assists!"

Not wanting to appear to be cocky, I gave the officer a slight smile as I shrugged my shoulders and threw my hands up. "That would be me!"

"Wow!" he said, even more wound up than the first time. "My boy loves you; he will be a freshman next year at Eastside High, and he's looking forward to following in your footsteps!"

I was flattered—that is, until he handed me a blank ticket and said "Here, sign this!" I hesitated before I reached my hand out. The officer, realizing what he had done, started laughing. "I'm sorry about that," he said as he scribbled "void" across the front of the ticket, "it's all that I have."

"I understand," I said, and I flipped the ticket over and signed my autograph. He then waved me off, but not before offering me a ride home. "No thanks, officer; that wouldn't look too cool with Mr. Basketball riding in the back of a police car!"

He laughed and said, "By the way, I'm Officer Green! Keep up the good work; it's so refreshing to see a young black male as a role model!"

I looked at Officer Green and said, "No, you keep up the good work! It's even more refreshing to see a cop not be so hard on a brother!" We both laughed as he pulled off.

I was a few blocks away from home when Jay pulled up in Jackie's Jeep. He rolled down the window, and a strong marijuana smell filled the air. His eyes were bloodshot and half closed; he was stoned! "Michael, get in; you're the one who's supposed to be driving, anyway. You know that I can't leave you out here. Besides, Ms. Betty and Nana would kill me if something happened to you."

I looked at my pitiful friend and realized it was all a setup. He had never wanted to hang out with me; he only wanted me to be the designated driver. I thought about what he had said, and he was right. Jackie had allegedly given him the keys to her truck because he had told her that I was going to drive. I would never have agreed to this setup had I known that Jay wanted to hang out with his new group of friends and get high. My conscience started bothering me, because Jay had absolutely no business being behind that wheel!

I thought about the drunken driving slogans that we plastered all around the school, like "friends don't let friends drive drunk," and I wondered if those slogans applied to being high also. I knew that I would never forgive myself if they went out and killed someone, all because I refused to drive. So, against my better judgment, I got ready to walk around to the driver side of the car so I could make Jay get out from behind the wheel. His homeboy in the backseat then rolled down the window (looking even more stoned than Jay, if that was possible) and said, "We don't need this goofy dude to drive us anywhere!" Jay and the other boy were so high they started cracking up laughing! I didn't think that it was funny at all; I thought that it was sad. That's when I realized that there was no way I was getting inside of that truck and jeopardizing everything that I had going for me just to try to save some lost souls; I would let God handle that. I looked at Jay and said, "I'll say a prayer for you." I ran the rest of the way home.

It was after ten when I finally made it inside the house. All of the lights were out, and I tried to be very quiet so that I wouldn't wake up Grandma Betty. That's when I tripped over my mother, Debbie, who was passed out drunk, lying in the middle of the doorway. "Arrrrrrgh," I moaned, because my ankle felt as though it were broken.

"Damn, John Michael, watch out!"

Once again, I ignored the fact that she called me John. I could barely help myself up off the floor, but I did, and I managed to hobble over to Debbie, who smelled like an entire bar. I tried to slide her across the room to the small couch that sat in the living room. She was extremely heavy, and as I proceeded toward the couch, dragging her by her arms, my ankle started throbbing. Before I knew it, it gave out, and Debbie and I both went crashing to the floor. The pain forced her to scream at me. "What in the hell are you trying to do to me? Are you trying to kill me?" she said, slurring with one eye open. She lifted her intoxicated body off of the ground and said, "I don't need no damn help; I can make it up those stairs by myself!" And she did it. It took her few a stumbles, a few falls, and a couple of missed steps before she finally disappeared into her room.

I tried on numerous occasions that night to make it up those same stairs, but I ended up conceding for fear of making my sprain a lot worse.

Grandma Betty exited the kitchen with her nurse's uniform on and a cup in her hand as I was sitting on the couch, trying to make myself move. "Good morning, Michael. Could you please go upstairs and take this black coffee to your mother? She needs to sober up before I drop her off at her AA meeting this morning."

"What's the point?" I said. Almost immediately, I regretted those words, because Grandma loved Debbie, and although my mother was an alcoholic, Grandma would never give up on her only daughter.

Grandma looked at me and said, "Son, when you have a bad habit that you really want to break, never quit quitting!

Shouldn't Debbie be the one saying this? I thought to myself, but it was as if Grandma read my mind when she sadly added, "And I won't quit quitting on my child!"

"I'm sorry," I said as I grabbed the cup and limped toward the stairs.

"Oh my goodness Michael, what happened to your leg?" Grandma said with a worried look on her face.

I looked down at it and said, "A little sprain, that's all." Grandma made me set the cup down, and she ran into the kitchen and came back with her first aid kit. She put some ice on my ankle to help with the swelling, and she bandaged it up extremely tight. She ordered me to stay off of it for at least twenty-four hours.

"Grandma, did you forget that I'm supposed to start basketball camp today? Coach should be here in ten minutes."

"Well, Mr. Basketball, you will just have to sit the next few days out, because that ankle doesn't look too good." She handed my guitar to me and said with a smile, "You might as well go to plan B today; that's always soothing." Then she grabbed the cup of coffee and marched up the stairs.

Grandma loved to watch me play basketball, but she hated to see me get hurt. I tried to explain to her that injuries are a part of the game. "Well, that's the part I don't like," she said. The first time that I played basketball and got hurt, I was in seventh grade. I was rushed to the hospital with a broken leg, and I had to wear a cast for six weeks. When I finally had my cast removed, Grandma sat me down and said, "Wouldn't you like to do something else that's a lot less dangerous?"

"I like the guitar," I said. The very next day she bought me a guitar and signed me up for singing lessons. Now, six years later—with the help of Coach, of course—I would be releasing my first demo in a few weeks. Grandma was so proud that she ultimately named my music career "plan B." I would love to call it "plan A," because that's where my real passion lies, but it won't get me a full scholarship to Michigan State University like my basketball career will.

When it came to basketball, I was really left with no choice. When I reached ninth grade, my height had shot up overnight; I was six-foot-three, and Coach was not taking no for an answer when I told him to let me think about it.

The doorbell rang, and I reached over to pick up my black case. As I tried to pull myself up, I came up short because of the bandage that was on my foot. Grandma then came rushing down the stairs to let Coach in.

※ ※ ※

Coach was in his early forties, and he stood at six foot five with a short, curly black afro with a few strands of gray sprinkled throughout. He was dark skinned with a muscular build, and he had very large hands that were permanently swollen from years and years of drug and alcohol abuse. He was a recovering addict (clean and sober for seventeen years). That's a part of his life that he did not mind sharing, because it was his full-time job to keep others from making the same mistakes that he made. He was a youth mentor and basketball coach, and if you asked him how he was doing, his answer was always, "One day at a time!"

He had been a part of this family and in my life since before I can remember. He and Debbie met at the treatment center over a decade ago. They dated for several years, each motivating the other, until Debbie decided being high on life just wasn't enough; she went to the bottle and hadn't kicked it since. Coach really cared for Debbie, but having been down that road for most of his adult life, he was determined to keep moving forward without her.

Since I had no idea who my father was, and Coach had no children of his own, he made himself my godfather; I was honored! Grandma Betty loved him also, and she treated him as if he were her son.

So there you have it; we were one big happy family, with the exception of Debbie and all of her setbacks.

✻ ✻ ✻

Coach entered the room and immediately went into concerned parent mode. "Mike, what's with the bandage?" I dreaded this conversation, because on the phone with him last night, I promised him that I wouldn't take Jay up on his offer and hang out with him. But I told Coach the basics, and from the disappointed look on his face, he already knew what had happened.

So I took a deep breath and told him the watered-down version of the story, because I didn't want him to be mad at Jay.

"Coach, after we talked on the phone, Jay called and asked if I was ready. I told him that I had basketball camp in the morning and that I would have to pass. He begged me, claiming that Jackie would not let him take the car unless I was going because she knows that I had a license. He said that we would only be out for a couple of hours, so I agreed."

Coach rubbed his chin and said, "Continue."

"Since he lives next door, I told him that it would only take me five minutes. When I knocked on the back door, he let me in, telling me to keep quiet because everyone was asleep. At that moment, a sinking feeling came over me."

"What was the sinking feeling?" Coach asked with anger in his voice.

"I don't believe Jackie really gave him the keys," I admitted. "It was a brand-new Jeep Grand Cherokee!"

"So let me get this straight; you guys stole her brand-new car?"

"I really wouldn't call it stealing; I guess you could say we borrowed it."

Coach looked at me really hard and said, "Michael! Ignorance is no excuse from the law; you guys stole the car!"

"Okay, if you say so," I said in a mild manner, wishing I could take back the entire conversation. "The moment we got inside the car, he asked me stop at the corner store so we could change places, as he wanted to drive. I wanted to bail out then, but I just didn't. We started listening to the demo CD that I made at the studio, and he really liked it. It had started out as a fun evening between two friends, but then he said he wanted his boys to listen to it. Ten minutes later, we pulled up on a block that I was unfamiliar with, and I started getting nervous. Jay saw the look in my eyes, and he said, 'Relax, homeboy; we will only be here for a few minutes.' Then he pulled out a joint!"

Coach had a worried look on his face, and I knew that it was time to put his mind at ease. "At that moment, Coach, your words played through my mind: 'Be your own man!' And that's just what I did; I swallowed my fears, threw him the keys, and sprinted two miles home through one of the roughest neighborhoods in the city of Detroit!"

I also told Coach about the drug addicts that were on the corner, and I told him about Officer Green. I left out the part about Jay and his boys laughing at me once they started smoking that weed; it would only have made our last conversation seem closer to reality than I wanted to admit. I knew that there was a point in life where you have to treat some friends like you do a poker hand: know when to hold 'em and know when to fold 'em. After that night, my fifteen-year relationship with Jay was seemingly coming to a bitter end.

Coach called my name, knocking me out of the stupor that I was in. "Is that it?" he asked.

I gave a long sigh and said, "No, that's not it!" I then continued telling Coach the rest of the story. "When I made it back home, I realized that I didn't have my keys, and I remembered where I had left them—on Jay's kitchen table! I had to knock on the door, and Nana Jackson wasn't too pleased with having a visitor that late in the evening. I am ashamed at what I had to do next."

Coach began to grow agitated.

"I lied to her," I said.

Coach breathed a sigh of relief.

"I told her that I was there to see Jay, because it was obvious that she didn't know he was gone. I grabbed my keys without her knowing and ran up to his room so I could cover for him. It broke my heart to look at her in the face and tell that bald-faced lie!"

"Well, son, loyalty sometimes comes at a cost," Coach said, beginning to lecture. "The question that you need to ask yourself is, is that cost really worth it?"

Wow! I had never thought of it like that.

—

Coach then asked, "Did you learn anything?" I was glad that he asked that question. I had learned three valuable lessons last night. "I thought about the drug addicts that were on the corner. When I asked God to remove them from that corner, Officer Green pulled up a few seconds later, and they ran; God really does come right on time. I also thought about how Officer Green praised me and called me a role model. I realized that, contrary to what we hear, there really are some good officers out there. And when it came to Jay and his friends, I realized that it's never wise to befriend people who brag about having nothing to lose; they normally live reckless or careless lives, and you just might find yourself getting caught in the crossfire."

Coach looked at me, and he had the biggest smile on his face when he said, "Impressive! Other than the lie, I am extremely proud of you! It took guts and courage to do what you did without caving into peer pressure, and I applaud you for that! Jay, on the other hand, I'm afraid is not the same person that you and I once knew! He is not that same kid that we used to play basketball with, go to baseball games, or go fishing with. That kid is long gone. I'm not saying that he will never come back around, but from what I see; he is lost and looking for an identity. He is becoming a follower, and you, Michael, are a leader; you proved that last night. And you know what leaders do?"

"What do they do, Coach? Tell me."

He smiled and said, "They get up, twisted ankle and all, and make it to basketball camp!"

I gave him a big hug because I knew he would listen and understand without being too judgmental. I felt like a heavy weight had been lifted off of my shoulders—and my ankle, because the pain seemed to have miraculously disappeared!

I said, "Help me up; it looks like we have camp to attend!"

Grandma Betty and Debbie had perfect timing, because they came down the stairs just as we were heading for the door. Coach looked at Debbie, and they exchanged pleasantries before he opened the door. As we all stepped onto the porch, we were all shocked by the flashing red and blue lights of police cars, a fire truck, and an ambulance all parked in front of Jay and his Nana's house! Panic and emotion got the best of me and Grandma Betty; without even thinking, we both took off for our best friend's house, with Debbie and Coach not far behind.

—

CHAOTIC

Big Man's last statement, "Don't get soft on me," gave me the confidence and the adrenaline rush that I needed. I took a deep breath, stuck my chest out, and headed for the stairs. I would prove to him that I was not soft and that I knew what loyalty meant—keep your mouth shut!

I'm sure Jackie knew what to do; she and Big Man had been through this many times before. The cops would burst into the club, looking for any illegal activity that they were possibly into; but they never could prove anything, because Big Man's juke joint was in a secret room in the basement, and no one ever told. Well, once again, they were wasting their time, because there was no evidence in this house—I had made sure of that.

As I started toward the stairs, I heard yelling and screaming. It was so loud that I couldn't make out whose voice was whose. I tried not to panic, because I knew that wouldn't do me any good! I was hoping that the cops were gone and that what I heard was just Jackie and Nana still going at each other's throats.

When I finally made it back to the scene, I couldn't believe my eyes; it felt as though a tornado had hit, because everything had spiraled out of control. Nana was on the speaker phone in hysterics, begging Uncle Scott to get here on the first flight out. "I'm scared," she said. "Jackie has lost it!"

One officer was on the radio, calling for an ambulance and backup, while the other officer was trying to restrain Jackie as she was cursing, yelling, screaming and acting like a deranged lunatic. "Get your damn hands off of me; I don't see a goddamn search warrant!" She was swinging her fists, kicking her legs, and going so wild and crazy that no one noticed I was standing there witnessing all of this. *Jackie sure made a mess this time*, I thought.

Jackie began breathing really heavy and fast until she was almost out of breath. When she caught a glimpse of me, she said in a very demanding and eager tone, "Shorty! Run!" Everything inside of me went numb as I realized they were here not for her, but for me. Uncle Scott screamed through the speaker at the same time as Nana; both were yelling "No!"

But it was too late, because I had already bolted for the top of the stairs; I really had no choice! There was no way I was going to get caught with the weed in my pockets; otherwise, they would really think I had helped to rob that gas station.

An officer who was hot on my trail yelled, "Don't do this; you will only make matters worse!" Right before I could reach the top of the stairs, he grabbed my leg, which made my size-twelve shoe land straight in his eye. He stumbled backward a few steps, and without thinking, I reached inside my pocket, trying to rid myself of the small packets. The next thing I knew, both officers had their guns pointed straight at me, and one of them screamed, "Take your hands out of your goddamn pockets before we blow your brains out!" When I realized what I had done—broken the number-one rule in a police situation: don't reach into your pocket—I snatched my hands out of my pockets so fast that the packets flew down the stairs like a Frisbee on a sunny day!

I yelled, "Please don't shoot; it was a mistake!" I honestly saw my life flash right before my eyes.

Nana sat there cradling Jackie; both women were nervous wrecks. Uncle Scott was still yelling into the speaker, saying, "Can the officer in charge please say something? What in hell is happening?"

The other officer tried to calm the situation and said, "Sir, I am Officer Green, and I am afraid that we are going to have to take this young man with us; he has a lot of explaining to do."

"Jay!" he screamed. I was still shaking, and I couldn't respond. "Answer me, dammit!" There was nothing that I could say; I had truly screwed up.

The officer had me laid out on the floor, and I was able to lock eyes with Jackie, who was growing weaker by the moment. I reached out to grab her hand, but an officer intervened by placing cuffs on my wrists. Jackie's eyes grew wider, and then all of a sudden she started gasping for breath even harder. I wanted to believe that she was reacting that way to protect me, but I knew better; she was clearly having an asthma attack. Nana nervously held Jackie tighter while dropping to her knees, and through tears she started praying for her, because Jackie didn't even own an inhaler—the doctors claimed that she had outgrown it.

A few minutes later, the paramedics, along with a couple of firemen, rushed in carrying a white stretcher and some sort of mask that they placed over Jackie's mouth and nose to stabilize her breathing. They picked her up and placed her on a stretcher. "Thank you, Jesus!" Nana rejoiced.

Seconds later, there was more banging on the door. I lay in my position quietly on the floor, assuming that it was my ride over to the hall of juvenile justice. The officer left me in a position behind the couch so I couldn't see the door, but when it flew open and people came crashing in, the situation went from bad to worse. I heard Michael, Ms. Betty, and Coach. I knew Michael all too well, and I knew that he had told Coach what had happened last night.

I prayed that the officers would not let them in, because if they did and Michael saw me in handcuffs, there was a good chance that he might mention last night. That frightened me even more, because if they questioned him about his whereabouts, he would surely incriminate himself. Although he was innocent, I wouldn't be able to live with myself if he had to be thrown into the middle of this chaos. I wouldn't want his scholarship or basketball career to be put in jeopardy because of me. The way I had treated him last night was wrong, so if it came down to it, I would do what I had to do and protect him by any means necessary.

MICHAEL'S DISAPPOINTMENT

We couldn't make it across that grass fast enough! We didn't see a fire, so we all leaned on the door and rang the bell. A cop swung it open so fast that all four of us fell inside just like a stack of dominoes!

Coach helped everyone up, and the cop said in a very firm tone, "This is strictly a police matter; do any of you live here?" Before we could respond, Nana Scott said, "It's okay, they're family." Then she fell into Grandma Betty's arms and started crying!

Nana Scott was helpless, and none of us knew what to make of the situation. Debbie ran over to Jackie, who had once been her best friend, and held her hand. Jackie was sitting on that stretcher looking so weak. She smiled at me and gave me a weak thumbs-up sign. The last time I had seen her, she congratulated me on becoming Mr. Basketball and gave me two $100 bills! "Go buy yourself those new Air Jordans and autograph them for me after your first game," she had said. Grandma Betty never allowed me to take money from Jackie or Big Man. "We don't need any handouts, Michael," she would say. I always honored her wishes, even though I knew that Jackie never meant it that way. Jackie knew how Grandma Betty felt about her lifestyle, but she had refused to take no for an answer. "It's okay, Michael, I cleared it with Ms. Betty," Jackie had said in a reassuring tone. And she had, too, because Grandma said that right after I played my first game in those shoes, I would be giving them right back to Jackie.

Seeing Debbie hold Jackie's hand like that made me feel a little jealous; I'd never known Debbie to have a compassionate bone in her body. She had never hugged me or congratulated me on anything. I tried to do everything to make her proud and possibly want to quit drinking and at least be my friend, but it never worked; she didn't like me and wanted nothing to do with me.

Grandma Betty had tried to make up excuses for Debbie by saying, "Michael, your mother's a sick woman; she doesn't mean any harm." After so long, those excuses had grown old and tired. When I became old enough, Grandma Betty had no choice but to sit me down and give me the full story on how I had come to be her responsibility.

✳ ✳ ✳

Grandma raised Debbie as a single parent after Grandpa died. Debbie was ten years old when they moved from Alabama to Detroit back in the 1970s because the job opportunities were better up north. When Grandma moved to Detroit's eastside; Nana Scott was the first person she met. She was the next-door neighbor, and since they both had small children at the time, they became fast friends. When Grandma worked, Debbie would stay with the Scotts, and when Grandma was off, Jackie would stay with them. Debbie loved this arrangement because, for her, Jackie was like the little sister she never had. They were both smart and pretty, and for the longest time, they did everything together.

Once they made it to high school, their relationship changed, because Grandma Betty sheltered Debbie and Debbie thought Jackie had the freedom to do whatever she wanted. This made Debbie envious because she was the oldest but Jackie had the most fun. Everyone really thought that they were sisters, and when Jackie began attending the same high school as Debbie, people started comparing the two. Yes, they both were pretty, but Debbie had a simple kind of beauty—smooth chocolate skin, light brown eyes, large dimples, and long hair that she kept in cornrows. She was somewhat plain. She really didn't have many friends because she wasn't allowed to hang out or go out on dates. She was thought of as a bookworm by her peers because she was so smart.

Jackie, on other hand, had it all: a knockout figure, an outgoing personality, and the attention of all the boys. Not to mention that she always turned heads wherever she went. Yes, Debbie still loved her, but she was so tired of being compared to her in school that she couldn't wait to go off to college so she could stop living in Jackie's shadow. Jackie, however, had no idea that Debbie felt this way.

According to Grandma, that's where things began to go wrong. Grandma Betty thought that being strict and sheltering Debbie had really paid off because she had gotten a full academic scholarship to Alabama State, and for that she was proud.

Little did Grandma know that Debbie had a very weak mind and could be easily influenced (because she had never had to think for herself; Grandma made all of her major decisions). And that's just what happened! Once she got to college and she had freedom, she went wild! She hooked up with the first man who told her she looked good, because no man had ever told her that before. She started hanging out, doing drugs, smoking cigarettes, and drinking. She flunked out her first semester, which ultimately made her lose her scholarship. She didn't care, because the only reason she had wanted to go away to school was to be on her own.

Every time she called home, she told Grandma that she was doing fine and she needed money for this project or that project, and Grandma just kept on sending it, thinking she was investing in her child's future. Little did she know that there was never going to be a future, because Debbie was using that money to get high and take care of the so-called man who claimed to love her—though she didn't even know his last name.

This went on for about eight months. Grandma knew nothing about it until she got a phone call late one evening from a hospital down in Alabama; something had happened to Debbie, and they asked her to get there quickly.

Grandma hopped on the first plane to Alabama. When she got to the hospital, they rushed her off to Debbie's room. Grandma couldn't believe her eyes! Her once beautiful, vibrant little girl who had held so much promise looked like a homeless woman who hadn't eaten or slept for days; Grandma almost couldn't recognize her. The closer Grandma stepped to Debbie, the more she blamed herself; she felt she had failed her daughter. She had been busy trying to protect her child from the outside world; she hadn't realized that all she had to do was prepare her for it.

The doctor asked Grandma if she would like to see the baby before social services put it into foster care. Grandma really couldn't comprehend what they were saying, because her head was still spinning, so the doctor repeated himself. "Ma'am, we found your daughter in an abandoned house, bleeding and high on drugs."

"What?" Grandma said.

"When the EMS brought your daughter here, she told us she was pregnant and she wanted us to get the bastard out of her stomach because she hated kids."

Grandma stared into space when the doctor said, "We had to call protective services because we can't send a child home if we feel that the baby will be in danger. She gave us your phone number and asked us not to mention the baby, but since you are her next of kin, we felt it was our duty and responsibility.

Debbie didn't care; she had already filled out the birth certificate and named me John Doe. Debbie put down John Doe as the father and signed over her rights just as soon as I came out of her womb. She said, "Now get that funny-looking kid out of my face!" (She thought that I was funny-looking, because I was a premature baby and weighed only three pounds.)

Once Grandma laid her eyes on me, there was no way that she was leaving me in Alabama. The doctor told Grandma that he saw cases like Debbie's all the time. "Beautiful, innocent college girl, first time away from home, hooks up with a local, takes some unknown drugs, and the next thing you know, they have lost it!" Grandma began crying. "Sometimes they find their way back; sometimes they don't," the doctor said. "Good luck, Ms. Stephens; I wish you the best." The doctor then walked away. There was nothing else he could do.

We all left the hospital and headed back to Detroit, against Debbie's will. That was over seventeen years ago, and my relationship with Debbie is still nonexistent.

✳ ✳ ✳

When the paramedics stabilized Jackie, Debbie was still holding her hand. My mind had drifted off, and I had no idea that I was standing in the way of the paramedics until Debbie said, very offensively, "John Michael, move out the way!"

It was like someone had lit a fire under me. Hearing her call me John—the name that she purposely put on my birth certificate because that's who she said I was conceived by—made me explode! "You know what, Debbie? I hate you too!" She froze still, as her face seemed to crumble into a million little pieces. She was so accustomed to me being passive that I really caught her off guard.

I knew that she had never wanted me, and her calling me that name was her way of reminding me of that. Grandma didn't have to share this story with me because every time Debbie would become inebriated, she proudly bragged about it because she thought it was funny. Luckily, Grandma changed my name to Michael Stephens as soon as she finalized the adoption when I was six months old. Debbie just wanted to make my life miserable because her life was—but not this time! I no longer wanted her love, affection, friendship, or approval; she had hurt me for the last time.

Grandma Betty looked at me but didn't say a word; she knew I had been holding this in for a long time. She rushed out the door behind the paramedics along with Nana Scott as Debbie stood there looking dumbfounded.

When the paramedics were gone, I was still clueless as to what had just happened until I overheard an officer talking to Uncle Scott on the speaker phone, giving him a play-by-play description of the situation. My stomach did somersaults when he said, "Mr. Scott, I respect your position, but I'm afraid your nephew will have to be detained. These are some very serious charges that he is facing. Accessory to an armed robbery at a gas station last evening, resisting arrest, and possession of a controlled substance. I looked at Coach because I couldn't believe what I was hearing. Coach didn't look alarmed at all. He knew, as his job required him to work directly with juveniles. That was why he had wanted to know in detail what I did last night.

An officer stepped behind the couch, and I was surprised to see it was Officer Green. He lifted Jay up by his elbows, and I saw that he was indeed handcuffed. He managed to lie there quietly the whole time, probably praying that we didn't see him in that compromising position.

Jay's uncle Scott tried to reason with the officer. He said, "I'm a high-powered attorney; could you please just hold off until I get there later on this evening? I promise I will straighten all this mess out then."

The Officer said firmly, "Sir, once again, I understand all of this, but just like you have a job to do, we as officers have a job to do as well. Now, you either send someone down to the Juvenile center this evening, or you can straighten this out when he has his hearing."

I grew nervous. Seeing my best friend in those handcuffs hurt me down to the core. I knew he had been acting out lately, but I didn't think he was capable of such a horrible act. I felt compelled to cover for my friend. The officer turned him around so they could make their way to the door, and I made eye contact with him. Out of desperation I opened my mouth, but before a sound could come out, Jay beat me to it. He yelled at me so loudly and ferociously that I nearly felt the house shake. "Michael, what the hell are you looking at? Haven't you ever seen handcuffs before? I don't like you. Now get the hell out of my house, Mr. Basketball."

I was growing furious; *first Debbie and now Jay?* When Officer Green realized who I was, he grabbed Jay's arms even tighter. He said, "Don't worry, you little punk; we're taking you to a place where you will meet new friends who are more on your level."

I was so angry that I wasn't going to take any more crap off of anyone else, including my best friend. I got ready to charge at him, but Coach's reflexes allowed him to catch me. He grabbed me in a bear hug and said, "Michael, let it go. It's for the best." I was hurt, because in the blink of an eye, our fifteen-year friendship was over. Just like a bad poker hand, it was time to fold 'em.

Uncle Scott was still on the other end of the speaker phone, listening to this final round of ruckus, when he shouted, "Officer, I think you're right. Book him."

TURMOIL

The look of rage on Michael's face when I maliciously attacked him was painful to watch. It seemed as though he had an out-of-body experience, and I am almost certain he would have knocked me flat on my back if Coach had not grabbed him. And I definitely would have deserved it. I felt horrible, because I had never even heard him raise his voice. Not only had he won Mr. Basketball, but he had also been nominated as one of the nicest people and most likely to succeed at Eastside High School. Thanks to me and Debbie, that all changed.

After Coach grabbed Michael, Coach looked at me and winked to show he agreed with me. I knew Michael didn't understand, but Coach did. He had been around for a long time and had worked with many troubled teens; he was determined not to let Michael or me become one of them. Sadly, I fell off course, and he had no choice but to keep it moving—with Michael, of course (at least that way he could save one of us). I knew he respected me for what I had done. After all, his words were imbedded in my head: "Always take accountability for your actions." And that's just what I did. Michael was now his top priority; Michael was so lucky to have someone like Coach in his life. I just hoped that I would get the chance to apologize before he took off for college in a few weeks.

My thoughts quickly turned from Michael to Jackie. I was afraid because she hadn't had an asthma attack in years, and for some reason this attack seemed different. She really didn't look like herself, and for the first time ever, I noticed that she had fear in her eyes. I was at a loss because she was my best friend, my rock, and my only hope to get out of this mess—because I could never do any wrong in her eyes. I knew she would be okay; it was just a matter of when. Jackie was strong and a fighter; a little thing like asthma couldn't keep her down—not for long, anyway.

It still felt bizarre, though, and for the first time in my entire life, I was alone. I had no one to call on that I hadn't let down. Tears formed in my eyes until Jackie's words came to my mind: "Shorty, boys don't cry." I sucked it up and thought about Big Man, who had no clue as to what was happening because he didn't like the police and refused to talk to them. "That's what lawyers are for," he would say. "If you pay them enough, they can make it go away." And that must be just what he did, because his troubles always seemed to disappear.

When the officer pushed me through the front door with my hands chained behind my back, I heard a loud thumping sound coming down the street. The officer and I both turned our heads in the direction of the loud music, and I couldn't believe my eyes. When I saw the big black Ram truck with the large antenna and tinted windows rolling down the street, it felt like this bad nightmare was finally coming to an end, because it was Big Man; he had finally shown up. Superman was here to save the day. But that hope and dream quickly faded as he slowly drove by the house, making as little eye contact with the police as possible.

At that moment I felt I was the one who needed an ambulance, because I thought I was about to die. I know that he saw me, because as the cops started stuffing me into the backseat, I caught a glimpse of him through his front window, and his eyes were focused on me. I wanted to yell, wave my hands, or do something crazy to get his attention, but it was no use; he kept right on driving.

When the police car drove off down the street with me in tow, I looked behind me, and there was his truck again; he had turned around. I grew anxious, thinking he was coming back for me. But I had no such luck. He had stopped in front of the house because Debbie was waving her arms back and forth, trying to get his attention.

My spirits were lifted a little, because at least he would now know what was going on, and I thought it might be only a matter of time before someone came and got me.

As we continued on our journey to the juvenile facility, the only thought that went through my head was what a day; Jackie was hauled off in an ambulance, and I am being hauled away handcuffed and in the back of a police car. Life sure isn't fair.

—

JUVENILE

———

Once we made it down to the Hall of Juvenile Justice, I was immediately ushered inside of the building and into a large cell with several other juveniles. Since it was my first time being detained and I had no clue as to what to expect, I asked to utilize the only right that I knew I had. "Can I please have my one phone call?"

The officer laughed along with the other inmates, and I couldn't figure out what was so funny until the officer said, "You have been watching too much TV; it doesn't work like that. We will make the call for you."

He gave me a piece of paper and told me to fill it out with the names and telephone numbers of my parents or legal guardians. He pretty much knew my circumstances, and he found it very humorous as I stared at the piece of paper.

My mind went blank. I couldn't think of one phone number, and even if I did, no one would answer, because they were both down at the hospital. I tried really hard to remember Big Man's phone number, but I knew it was no use because I hardly ever dialed it. I thought about my grandfather, Big Man's dad, and wondered how I could get in touch with him. Every month, he sent me money and a postcard from a different part of the country; I knew that he would come to my rescue. After staring at the piece of paper for several seconds, I knew that it was no use; I had to just face the fact that I had nobody I could call.

When the officer noticed my hesitation, he decided to taunt me and say, "What's wrong, tough guy; you need your phone book?" And he held up my cell phone in a little plastic baggie. My mind started spinning. I now knew what had made them come looking for me; I had dropped my cell phone outside of that gas station. I felt like a complete idiot. Here I was thinking that Michael would talk too much and incriminate us both; but come to find out, he didn't have to incriminate us—because I already had.

When I entered the cell there were some young guys staring at me. Their faces looked very familiar, but since I wasn't there to make any friends, I tried my best to act tough and pay their sharp daggers no mind. Instead of staring back, I focused my attention on the clock on the wall, which read 11:30. I was wondering how long was it going to take Big Man to come and get me, since I knew that Uncle Scott was in California and there was no way he would be here anytime soon.

I sat on the hard bench and buried my head in the palms of my hands. I soon heard someone call my name. I started to get nervous, because there were no officers around. *I haven't been in this place five minutes, and I'm already being picked on,* I thought. When he said my name again, I had no choice but to answer. "Whassup," I said in the toughest voice I could muster.

When he stood up and walked over to me, I was taken aback, because it was Max. He had two black eyes and a busted lip, and his jaw looked like it had been knocked out of place; he looked nothing like himself. "What in the hell happened to you?" I asked nervously. I looked at the other two guys that were standing there, and I hoped and prayed that they hadn't done that to him, because if they had, I didn't stand a chance.

He tried to put on a brave face when he said out of the side of his mouth, "It happened last night." I didn't know the full story of what happened, but looking at him, I was very eager to find out. He spoke very slowly because of the pain that he was in, but I didn't mind, because I didn't want to miss even one detail.

"Jay, me and Marcus screwed up big time." I started to break out into a cold sweat, because I had been with them last night and I didn't understand what he meant. I listened very closely because I was desperate and didn't want to end up like him, so I let him finish without any interruptions.

He went on to say, "When we all headed for that gas station, we didn't know that they had just gotten robbed and the police were already en route. We only wanted to buy some smokes, and when the clerk asked for ID, we didn't have any. He then asked us to put them back and leave. Marcus refused to leave without them smokes, and he snatched the entire carton out of the clerk's hand without paying, and that's when the clerk jumped from behind the counter and kicked me in the face, knocking me down. Marcus panicked and pulled out the gun that he always carried, and that's when the clerk pulled out his and fired shots at us, hitting my brother in the leg—he claimed self-defense. When the police arrived, he blamed the robbery from earlier on us since we both had guns. They said that we had come back to finish the job. They looked at the surveillance tape and saw all three of us heading for the gas station, and when you ran back to the car to get your wallet, they assumed that you were the getaway driver. They tried to get me to cough up your name, but hey, I'm no snitch. I told them that I had no idea who they were talking about, but that was when he found your phone lying right there on the ground."

I must have looked like a deer caught in the headlights, because I was beyond frightened; I was petrified. "Max, I didn't know that you and Marcus carried guns."

He looked at me and said, "Have you seen the neighborhood that we live in? Everyone carries a gun. There's a lot that you don't know about us."

I was absolutely sick to my stomach because I finally understood what Uncle Scott had tried to tell me a long time ago: "Be careful of the company that you keep." I had only met Max and Marcus a couple of weeks before in the principal's office before I got kicked out of school. I had thought that they were cool people; I guess I was wrong.

The more Max kept talking, the less and less I heard him, because my mind was still stuck on the surveillance tape; I couldn't believe that I had gotten caught up in this much trouble.

He then asked me if my family was on their way down to get me. I said, "Yes, my dad should be here real soon."

He said, "Well, you better hope so, because the courts close around four. If he doesn't make it down here before then, you will have to stay the night here and see the judge first thing in the morning like I did."

Now I really didn't understand what was going on. I needed some clarity on what he had just said. "You mean to tell me that you have already seen the judge? Why are you still here? What about your mom? She's just going to leave you here in this place?"

He looked at me and said, "Damn, man, you really are an amateur at this, huh?" I didn't realize how stupid I must have sounded. He shut me up really quickly when he said, "My mom wasn't with me when I did the crime." I wish I had just kept my mouth closed, because lately it seemed that every time I opened it, I inserted my foot into it.

"It's cool, man," he said, trying to put me at ease as he continued on with the story. "After the incident, the cops took my brother to the hospital, and they brought me down here. They couldn't get in touch with my mom because she works midnights and doesn't get home until seven in the morning. Once they got in touch with her this morning, they told her that I had a hearing down here at nine and that she had to be present or the outcome could be far worse. When I made it into the courtroom, she wasn't there, and I didn't believe she was going to make it. The judge was so irritated that she was getting ready to throw the book at me, but then my mom finally showed up—thirty minutes late. She had to go down to the hospital first and check on Marcus. I was so happy when I saw her storm through those doors, but when she approached the bench; I wasn't expecting to hear what came out of her mouth. She didn't even look at me or ask me what happened or who was at fault; she just started crying. She didn't even give the judge time to explain the case before she started calling herself a failure, a bad parent, and an ignorant person for being a single mother trying to work hard to care for two teenage boys without any help from the state or our deadbeat dad.

"Man, I never knew she felt that way. She is a very good mother; it's just that me and my brother like the designer labels that she can't seem to afford. Instead of stressing her about it, we just go out and try to make it happen for ourselves. I mean, we never killed anybody. I wish I could have told her that I was sorry and that she was a great mother, but she wasn't trying to hear it; she was so busy tearing herself down that the judge couldn't even get a word in." Max became so bummed out thinking about his mom that he didn't even want to finish the story.

I didn't know if I was going to insert my foot in my mouth again with the next question, but I needed him to finish the story, so I asked him, "So did the judge finally get a chance to speak?"

He giggled a little because he knew I was scared, and then he said, "Yeah, she did. The judge said that she understood my mom's struggle and told her that she was sure that she did the best she could for us. She also told her it is unfortunate that children don't seem to appreciate the sacrifices single parents make to love, care for, and provide for them. Then the judge had the nerve to say, 'Well, Ms. Smith, today must be you and your son's lucky day, because I am not going to throw him away like I was planning on doing before you came. I am going to help you out. I am going to give this young man another shot at possibly becoming a decent, productive, human being.'

Max was steadily shaking his head as he told this part of the story, and I started getting wound up just listening to him. He was taking too long to finish the story, and I was afraid that Big Man would arrive and I might never know what happened to him, so I said, "Man, why are you still here?" I really don't think that I was ready for what he had to say; because what he said next sent me right back into the miserable state that I was previously in.

He looked at me and said, "This is it."

I looked around and said, "This place is it?"

He said "The judge seems to think that in about a year and a half, I should be all straightened out, disciplined very well, and caught up in school—after I complete the six-month boot camp and a year of training at a juvenile facility up in northern Michigan.

It still didn't make sense to me, so I said "Man, I'm no lawyer, but isn't that kind of fast? It just happened last night, and they're sending you away just like that?"

He cleared his throat and said, "Naw. There's more to it than that."

Once again I gave him my undivided attention. "Me and my bro were both already on probation for stealing cars, armed robbery, and little stuff like that. Part of my probation was that I had to stay out of trouble, stay in school, do community service, and I was supposed to sit inside of the courtroom and listen to some criminal cases and do a report on them. I didn't do any of that stuff, and my probation officer had warned me that when she caught up with me, it wasn't going to be nice. She wanted me to turn myself in. Well, I guess she got her wish." He said this like it was his probation officer's fault that he was in trouble. This was unbelievable. *What part of what he just told me does he think is little?* I thought to myself. This was some serious stuff. I was really riding around with some hard-core thugs. He then said, "Well, at least I made out better than Marcus; he's eighteen, and he more than likely will be sent to a state prison. It's a mandatory two years for just having a gun," he said, shaking his head.

"Aw man, I know that devastated your mom. Jackie would have probably beaten that judge up right there in her courtroom."

He said, "You're not going to believe this, but my mother was actually happy; she thanked the judge. I'm still trying to figure out whose side she was on."

After he saw the blank expression on my face, he said, "Don't worry, Jay; since all they did was find your cell phone, Judge Kemp may let you off easy." I nodded. Because I didn't have the guts to tell him that I had made more trouble for myself, I just let it go.

A few hours later, the guard opened the cell, and I stood up because I just knew Big Man had come to rescue me. I was wrong; an officer was there to take Max to his new home. I sadly waved good-bye; the time was 3:15 p.m.

The clock slowly ticked away. When four o'clock came and went; my hopes of seeing Big Man and not having to spend the night there were gone. In an instant, my life had changed from being a spoiled little rich kid to a lost, lonely juvenile delinquent. I was frustrated, and this was one of the lowest points in my life. And to think that I thought living in California with Uncle Scott was bad; that idea seemed like heaven right about now. I never realized how fast a person's life could drastically change. I knew that I had let a lot of people down, especially earlier that day, but I didn't think I deserved to be treated like a caged animal. If they wanted me to learn a lesson, well, lesson learned, because I never wanted to see the inside of a jailhouse again.

After another few hours went by, I came to the realization that Jackie was still in the hospital, because never in a million years would she make me suffer like this.

There was another jingling of keys, and when I looked up, the clock read 7:15 p.m. It was another officer I hadn't seen before; they had changed shifts, and I was still here. He came in, did roll call, and slid three trays of what I presumed was dinner under the door. I took one look at the stale piece of bread, the dried-out turkey, and the cold mashed potatoes and tossed it right in the trash. I ate the apple and drank the juice before I balled up in a knot and forced myself to fall asleep. It was evident that I wasn't leaving anytime soon.

I tossed and turned the whole night. The bed was hard; I had a thin, smelly blanket; and on top of that, I smelled bad. I stared at the clock every hour on the hour. Daybreak seemed like it took forever to arrive.

At 6:00 a.m. an officer opened the cell screaming and yelling our names, startling everyone. We all jumped up like there was a fire. *Hell, I just dozed off,* I thought. His yelling really was unnecessary, since the cell was not big at all. He rolled in mop buckets and clean linen for the bunks. I grabbed my things and moved out of the way.

The officer looked at me and started yelling "What in the hell are you doing? This ain't the damn Marriott; now get to cleaning. This place stinks!" He pushed the bucket toward me, causing it to spill over, soaking my socks and the bottom of my jeans.

"Yuck," I said. I quickly grabbed the mop and started slinging the water, all the while praying that I wouldn't throw up from the disgusting smell.

After we finished with the chores, the officers fed us a cold breakfast and told each of us to gather up our things because we had to be in court at 9:00 a.m. The word "court" had me frightened; I wondered how I was supposed to face that judge alone. "Excuse me, officer," I asked, "but has anyone gotten in touch with my parents?"

He looked at me and said, "That's normally how it goes," like I knew what that was supposed to mean. Before I could ask the next question, he cut me off. "Look, everyone gets to ask me one question, and you just did." *What kind of stuff was that,* I thought. *He didn't even answer it.* "I guess you should have thought about that before you went looking for trouble," he said in a nasty tone.

I let it go. I was just happy that I would finally be leaving my cell.

I grabbed my shirt from my bunk and what I thought were my brand-new Air Jordan shoes from under the bed and proceeded to get dressed. I bent over to put my shoes on and noticed that they were ripped and had an awful smell coming from them. I was thinking that maybe a rat had somehow gotten a hold of my shoe and bitten a hole in it, but then I noticed the guy that was in the bunk next to mine; he was wearing my shoes. He looked me up and down as if daring me to say a word. I thought about it, but I didn't. I put the smelly shoes on, and once again I felt like throwing up.

When 8:30 a.m. rolled around, the officer told all three of us to gather up all of our belongings and line up along the wall. I asked for a toothbrush, but the officer shot that request down, saying, "Having a toothbrush is a privilege."

They chained all of us together, and we were finally on our way to the courtroom.

Once we had all exited the elevator, the officer removed the chains and we were standing in front of the courtroom door, which read "Honorable Judge Rhonda Kemp." I realized that was the same judge Max had appeared before. It was a brand-new day, and my bad luck still hadn't changed. I hoped and prayed that someone would be in that courtroom for me, because I couldn't stand another day sleeping in those deplorable conditions.

Judge Kemp

I was the first name called in the courtroom. When I entered, there was no Jackie, Nana, or Big Man; instead, there was Uncle Scott— the last person that I expected to see. Uncle Scott was standing across from the judge's bench with a stone-cold face; there were plenty of things that he didn't like, and being inconvenienced was one of them.

The guard walked me over and positioned me right next to him. I was too ashamed to face him, so I stared straight ahead and focused my attention on the empty bench. Uncle Scott was heated. He firmly grabbed my shoulders and turned me around so that I could make direct eye contact with him. Since the judge hadn't entered the courtroom, he took advantage of the opportunity and gave me a good tongue lashing. "Is this the life that you really want to live? Is this the path you really want to go down? Was it all worth it?" He never gave me a chance to answer one question before he started firing more questions at me. The only response that I could come up with was "No, sir."

The bailiff suddenly interrupted by saying, "All rise." The judge had finally taken the bench. The expression on her face was serious. I was sworn in, and Uncle Scott introduced himself. She looked at Uncle Scott and said, "I'm aware of who you are, Mr. Scott. I had no idea that you handled juvenile cases." She appeared to be confused. He looked at the judge and said, "Well, Your Honor, under most circumstances, I don't; but when it's your nephew that you helped raise, you really don't have a choice."

She looked at him and smiled. "I clearly understand."

That smile was quickly turned upside down when she looked over my file. "Wow, he's been a very busy young man these past couple of days." Uncle Scott stood silent, and I lowered my head. "Maybe you could use a little break, and the courts can take him off your hands for a little while. A change of scenery does everyone some good, especially when they are this young," she said without blinking an eye.

Uncle Scott's response was, "I couldn't agree with you more."

My entire body started quivering because I thought about Max and what he was probably doing right about now—suffering. I was not going to stand silent and let them keep me in this place without a fight. If they wanted humility, then I could show them humility. "Please, please, please, I'm so sorry; I was running with the wrong crowd, and I know this now. Just give me another chance, and I promise I will never even walk by this place again in my life." I knew it was a stretch, but I was desperate.

I was hoping that she would feel sorry for me, but the minute I said "wrong crowd," she grabbed her gavel and slammed it down hard on the bench before yelling, "Hold it. Young man, I don't allow swearing in my courtroom." I had to back track the words in my head because I just knew that I hadn't said a curse word; I wasn't that stupid.

"It's obvious that you don't understand what you just said, so let me give you the rules. If you want to say you're sorry, then say that you're sorry. If you want to say that it won't happen again, then say that it won't happen again. What you won't do is blame others for your actions. What you won't say is that you were hanging with the wrong crowd. I have only one thing to say about people who use that excuse about the wrong crowd: young man, you *are* the crowd."

Once again I thought, *Open mouth; insert foot.* I was embarrassed, but I still was not giving up. I humbly said, "I'm sorry, and it will never happen again."

Uncle Scott raised his hand and asked the judge if he could speak. She nodded. I closed my eyes as he started speaking, because I wanted to take my mind to another place. I was skeptical when he said to the judge, "We have a very serious family matter that has to be attended to immediately. I just wanted to ask the courts if my nephew, Jayson Lee Jackson II, could be released under my supervision temporarily, since he has never been in any trouble with the law."(How clever of Uncle Scott to think of that one. That's what I love about lawyers; they know when to play their trump card.) I held a straight face because I didn't care what he said; I just wanted out.

The judge looked at him and said "Mr. Scott, I have no problem releasing him under your supervision; however, the courts are going to recommend that he be put on probation and an electronic monitoring device for six months. This device would monitor his whereabouts, give him a curfew, and make sure he goes to school."

Uncle Scott said, "That sounds fair." The next question caught me off guard. "Would it be a problem if we change his probation to a different state?" I kept a straight face, hoping that she would say no.

She then asked, "What state are you talking about, Mr. Scott?"

"California," he said. The judge smiled once again and said, "I guess he will get that change of scenery after all."

HOME

—

After about forty-five minutes, the paperwork was signed and I was released. The only stipulation was that I had to report to the courts in California within thirty days to get fitted for my electronic monitoring device.

I agreed and signed the paperwork so I could be released, but I had no plans of moving to California.

Once we made it to the front of the courts, Uncle Scott's limo driver was waiting. He opened the back door for the both of us, and we got in. The air conditioner was blowing at full speed, and the cool air felt good on my skin, but Uncle Scott reached over and turned off the air, opting to roll down the windows. I assumed the funk coming from under my arms was too much for him to bear. I looked at him and said, "That bad, huh?"

He turned to me and said, "Worse," and started fanning the air. "Jackson, your Nana, Jackie, and I really need to talk to you about a serious matter." I looked at him because I already knew what that matter was—me moving to California. I sat quietly because I knew that unless they threatened Jackie with a gun, she wasn't going to agree to something like that. He said, "We should be on our way down to the hospital, but there's no way that I'm going to take you there smelling and looking the way that you do. We are on our way to the house so I can make some phone calls and some arrangements, and so you can clean yourself up."

I looked at him and asked, "Hospital? Why is she still in the hospital?" He looked at me but didn't answer the question. Instead he tapped on the limo driver's window and told him to pull in to the closest McDonald's so we both could grab a bite to eat.

—

Uncle Scott ordered a large coffee, and I ordered pancakes and sausages. I had taken only a few bites of my food when he looked at me and said, "What's the matter; did they feed you too much in that place?" I turned toward the window without even answering, because thoughts of Jackie still being in the hospital were enough to make me lose my appetite.

We pulled up to the house, and he said in his military voice, "You have less than thirty minutes," as he looked down at his watch to let me know that I was being timed. Man did I need a nice joint right then; it was going to be tough dealing with him. "Before I clean up, can I please go in the back and check on my dog, Bruiser? I know that his bowl is empty, and he probably needs some water."

He looked at me and said, "All right, but you better start looking for a new home for him; he's not coming to California."

Why the heck would I want to torture my dog by living with you? I thought. "Okay," I said, and I ran toward the gate, punched in the code, and entered the backyard.

Bruiser started barking as soon as he saw me. I knew that all the police commotion must have frightened him, because he was very happy to see me. The moment I grabbed him, he started licking my face. I put some fresh water in his bowl, and I went into the shed and grabbed the shovel and his dog food.

Once I had filled his bowl with the food, I looked behind his doghouse, and there it was—Jackie's black bag. It was still locked. I had no idea what the combination to the lock was; and it was a good thing that I didn't, because I would have taken another few packs of the weed out and blazed one right here in the backyard.

I quickly grabbed the shovel and started digging a deep hole inside of Bruiser's doghouse. I knew her bag would be safe there, because even if I had to get rid of Bruiser, there was no way that anyone would tear down his doghouse; Big Man had gotten it custom built for me to house my dog in.

I heard Uncle Scott yell, "Jackson, what are you out there doing? It shouldn't take you that long."

Sweat started pouring down my face, because I had to hurry before he came back there. I yelled, "I'm just shoveling up his poop."

"Well, hurry up, because we don't have all day."

"Yes sir."

The hole was about two feet deep—just big enough to drop the bag inside without being noticed. I shoveled some of the dirt on top of the bag and grabbed two cement slabs that were outside the doghouse and covered the hole with them. I then topped the cement off with more dirt.

I rushed into the house, removed my shoes at the front door, and ran up the stairs so I could get ready. It took me fifteen minutes to get showered and dressed, and when I realized that I didn't have any money I went into Jackie's room to look for some. When I stepped inside of her room, it looked nothing like I had left it. Someone had been in there, because her closet door and dresser drawer were open, her bed was messed up, and a few of her shoe boxes had been thrown around. I surveyed the room very carefully, and since nothing appeared to be missing, I continued looking for some loose cash lying around. I found nothing inside of her dresser but a half a pack of cigarettes. Since I knew she wouldn't need them, I helped myself to them. I knew that I wouldn't be able to smoke them right away, but as soon as Uncle Scott let me out of his sight, I was going to smoke the entire pack.

Since there wasn't any money lying around her room, I decided to check one last place—her mattress. I lifted up her mattress, and there lay the small .22 caliber handgun that Big Man made her carry for protection because she often handled a lot of money when she left the bar. I stared at the gun and wondered if it really was a "peacemaker," as he claimed it was. I didn't touch it, because that's the only thing that Jackie said was off limits. "It's only for protection, Shorty," she had said to me. I moved a few papers around before I found an envelope labeled "bills." It had $560 in it, so I slipped out $60 and left the rest; there was no way I could justify having all of it around Uncle Scott.

After I put the $60 in my pocket, I made up her bed and tried to tidy up her room. Uncle Scott soon called my name from the bottom of the stairs and said "Let's go, Jackson," sounding like the military drill sergeant he had once been.

"Yes, sir." Man, is that phrase going to take some getting used to, I thought.

When I finally made it back outside, I looked over at Michael's house. He and Coach were leaving with suitcases in their hands. Michael didn't even look my way. Coach waved to Uncle Scott and me as he and my once best friend drove down the street. I felt like crap.

As we settled back inside of the limo, I asked, "If Jackie is still in the hospital, then who was in her room messing with her things?"

Uncle Scott said, "Oh, I didn't get a chance to tell you, but your dad was by here last evening, and he was worried about you both. He said that he sent someone down to the juvenile center to check on you, but they wouldn't release any information to non–family members. He said that he would have done it himself but that he doesn't have a very good reputation with the police. I'm very familiar with his lifestyle, so I told him not to worry about you; you needed some time to think about what you had done anyway. I told him to shift his focus to his wife, because she needed his support far more than you did. So I let him go up to her room and grab some things that he felt would make her hospital stay more comfortable."

I couldn't believe my ears; they both had purposely left me there. "So is he there with her now?" Uncle Scott hunched his shoulders before he said, "I have no idea." I felt disappointed that Big Man would leave me in such a terrible place. Jackie had always done everything in her power to make sure that she, Big Man, and I were a team, and now that she was ill, Big Man was showing his true colors—he really didn't give a damn about me. His only concern was Jackie, and that hurt. I couldn't wait until I saw Jackie; I was going to make sure that I let her know what Big Man had done.

HOSPITAL

I was quiet during the entire fifteen minutes it took for us to get to the hospital. The driver let us out in front of the building. I jumped out of the car so fast I nearly slammed the door shut on Uncle Scott's leg. I ran to the front desk and asked for Jacqueline Jackson's room. The clerk said that she was only allowed two visitors at a time and that both passes were taken. The clerk picked up the phone so she could dial Jackie's room, and just then I spotted Nana walking down the hall, holding on to Ms. Betty like her life depended on it.

I sprinted ten steps up to Nana, and when she saw me, she tried to straighten herself up, but it was too late; I had already seen the tears. I reached out to her as she reached out to me, and we both collapsed into each other's arms. Uncle Scott came from behind, and we all had one big group hug. Nana then looked at me and said, "Let's hurry, Jay; she's been asking for you all day."

"No," I protested, "I need to be alone with her."

Before Nana could utter another word, Uncle Scott jumped in and said, "Let the boy go."

She then handed me the pass, which read "room 428." She pointed in the direction of the elevators and said, "It's elevator B." Before I took off, she said, "Jay, your father's up there also." That caught me off guard; I really wasn't prepared to see him at the moment. All of my unanswered questions had to be put on the back burner for now; Jackie was my only concern.

I nervously walked down the hall. When I spotted the gift shop, I took the sixty dollars that I had and grabbed two balloons that read "Get Well Soon" and two red roses. I then followed the dreary hallway around to elevator B. I stepped onto the elevator, and it was like a brand-new world. The atmosphere had changed from dull and dingy to bright and bold. And it didn't stop there. The fourth floor looked like heaven, with pink-and-white fluorescent walls, hand-painted Bible scriptures, and signs that read, "Hope, Love, and Peace." I had never seen a hospital so beautiful and serene before. If I were Jackie, I wouldn't want to leave this place either, I thought. There's no telling when the last time she had this much rest was, and there is no telling when she will get it again. So she better take advantage of this.

When I looked down at my visitor's pass to read the room number on it, I bumped into two glass double doors that read "Women's Cancer Treatment Center." I did a double take. *I must be on the wrong floor,* I thought. I was getting ready to find the nurse's station when a beautiful nurse who had just walked out of a patient's room said, "Can I help you find someone?" I couldn't open my mouth. She took the pass out of my hand and said "Mrs. Jackson—what a very elegant lady, even in hospital gear."

I looked at her and said, "She's in here for asthma. Why is she on this floor?" The nurse gave me a puzzled look and quickly led me to room 428, where there was a beautiful pink sign on the door that read, "outside this door is where the sorrow ends and the fighting begins," and Jacqueline Jackson was the name underneath.

She looked at me and said, "I'm so sorry, young man; it's not every day that a visitor comes up here unprepared. If there's anything that the team and I can do for you, please don't hesitate to ask."

Breast cancer? I thought. There has to be some sort of mix-up. This type of disease doesn't happen to women like Jackie; she is still young and full of life. No, I wasn't going to accept this.

I wanted to ask the nurse to take it back. That's what I needed—for her to take it back. She saw the disillusionment on my face and quickly left me alone.

The door was cracked a little, and I hesitated before I peeked inside. I heard Big Man on the phone, but I could only make out part of his conversation. He said to the person on the other end, "I know that we were supposed to close the deal last week, but we had a minor setback. Please don't sell the property to the other bidder; my wife and I have been waiting so long to get this project off the ground. She had to leave town for a few days, and when she comes back, we will have the two-hundred-thousand-dollar check for you, along with the signed contract." I gasped because I couldn't believe my ears; Big Man had actually referred to Jackie's cancer as a minor setback, and he was actually still thinking about opening up a new spot at a time like this, the selfish bastard.

I was so mad that I burst into the room, and I was stopped dead in my tracks. Jackie lay there peacefully as the cancer was taking its toll on her body. There were no fancy wigs, long lashes, or tapered eyebrows; they had all been replaced by a tube in her nose and a heart monitor next to her bed. Once again, I gasped. This startled Big Man, who was sitting next to her. He abruptly ended the call with "Give me a few hours," not sure how much of his conversation I had overheard.

He stood up and gave me a big bear hug as though he hadn't seen me in years. I did not reciprocate. I stiffened my body up like a board because I was angry. Once he noticed my resistance, he patted me on my shoulders and started wiping tears from his eyes. I decided to hold off on mentioning his conversation; this was all about my Jackie now.

"Did you know?" I said in the coldest voice I could find.

He looked at me very apologetically and said, "She made me promise not to tell; said we were going to beat this."

I walked over to her bed and grabbed her hand; she felt so soft. Big Man was still talking to me, but his voice soon faded out once my eyes landed on Jackie. She was dressed to kill, even in the hospital. She wore a designer pink silk scarf with matching pajamas, giant diamond studs in her ears, and a gold-encrusted cross around her neck. That explained why Big Man had messed her room up—to make sure that she was at her finest. I kissed her hand, hoping that she would at least open her eyes, but she didn't budge.

I looked at Big Man and said, "How long has she been out?"

He said, "Do you know what's so funny, Shorty?" I wasn't in the mood for any guessing games, and I didn't see how he could find anything funny at a time like this, so I sat quietly. "I have been up here half the night and most of the day, and she hasn't woken up for me once." He looked very disappointed.

"That's strange," I said. "Nana just told me that she has been asking for me all day."

He sighed and said, "I heard. It seems like everyone has had a chance to speak with her except for me. I have been praying all day for her to say something to me, but so far I haven't had any luck. Her doctor said that once her medication wears off, she will come to."

—

I looked at him and said, "Well, I'm not leaving here until she does come to." He kept looking at his watch like he had someplace important to be, so I said, "Why don't you go and take a break. When she wakes up, I promise that you will be the first person I call."

He stood up and paced the floor, looking like he had something heavy on his mind. I continued looking at Jackie while holding her limp hand. Big Man said, "Shorty, have you by any chance seen Jackie's black bag? I went by the house last night and couldn't find it anywhere; there are some very important papers that I need out of there."

I said, "Ye—" before I felt Jackie squeeze my hand with as much pressure as her frail body could muster.

His whole demeanor changed, and he seemed anxious. "Did you say yes? Do you know what she did with it?" Before I could answer again, she squeezed even tighter, and I knew right then that she was trying to tell me something.

I didn't know what she was trying to tell me, but I knew I needed to get him out of there before he caught on. So I said yes again so he wouldn't get suspicious. "She took it with her when she left the house the other day. She said something about going to her new place; did you look there?"

His facial expression went blank, and I had to admit to myself that I was enjoying this part. I decided to deliver a gut-wrenching blow. "You know what? Come to think of it, I saw her put it in a box and address it to Switzerland; we dropped it off at the post office the other day," I said, like it was no big deal.

His eyes grew wide, and he said, "Huh." His phone started ringing, and he mumbled a few bad words as he leaned over to kiss Jackie. "Please call me as soon as she wakes up," he said as he was exiting the room.

I might as well top it off, I thought to myself. "Okay, Dad." He looked back at me like I had lost my mind, because I had never called him that. Big Man headed out the door rubbing his forehead.

After Big Man left, I took the roses that I had and placed them under her nose—Jackie loved the smell of roses. That's when a tear rolled down her cheek as she struggled to open her eyes. I promised myself that I wouldn't show any emotion; Jackie needed me to step up and be strong. I didn't let go of her hand or take my eyes off of her as she started blinking really fast, trying to focus on me.

Staring at Jackie's once lively spirit, I wondered how long she had been keeping this awful disease a secret and whether she would ever be able to live a normal life again.

I whispered in her ear, "Jackie, he's gone; please say something."

She stared at me for a really long time before she opened her mouth and tried to make a sound; nothing came out. She had a look of agony on her face. I felt helpless; she appeared to be in so much pain. I was getting ready to press the button for the nurse when she made a hissing sound. "Sssssssssssssssss." I had no idea what was happening until she made it again. "Ssssssssss." Finally, she used every bit of breath in her body to make the word "Son" come out.

That caught me off guard. I shook my head really hard and extremely fast as I said, "No, Jackie … I mean yes … I mean no … It's me, Shorty." I got scared. She was not in her correct state of mind. She had never called me son, and I didn't want her calling me that—not under these circumstances. I needed her to keep fighting. The cancer was winning; and it showed, because it was doing all of the talking...

Another tear rolled down her cheek as she slowly and quietly whispered the words "I'm Sorry." I started shaking my head again because I had no idea what she was sorry for. I took my finger and put it over my mouth and said, "Shh," but she was not taking no for an answer; she was persistent.

It was no use in trying to fight with her now. I just prepared myself for whatever she had to say, as long as she wasn't talking about giving up. Patience was my new best friend. I placed my face as close to hers as possible, and she started speaking in a low, raspy voice. "I'm sorry for being your friend and not your mother. I was selfish, immature, irresponsible, and so wrong. When the cops took you away, it was entirely my fault; I should never have told you to run. I have stolen so many opportunities from you, and I don't think I can ever forgive myself." I continued shaking my head as she continued to slowly speak. "Please, son, I'm begging you. Listen to your Nana. Move to California with your uncle and make something of yourself."

Tears started to fill my eyes, and my heart began to sink. She tried her best to lift her weak arms up to wipe my tears, but she had no energy to do so. At that moment, I hated this mean disease that I knew so little about. She then used every breath that she had to clear her mind and conscience. "I want you to be better than me and Big Man. I have been holding on just to tell you this. Please forgive me." Her words started to become fainter as she tried to catch her breath. "I want you to take that black bag and get rid of my medicine and put the rest away. It's all yours—all three hundred thousand dollars. Don't, under any circumstance, give it to Big Man." Her words were now barely above a whisper. "It's all that I have to give you. I love you, Shorty. And again, I'm soooo sorry."

Those words stung like a bee, and there was nothing that I could do about it. Jackie was giving up. There was no way that I would let her continue to badger herself, because through my eyes, she was the best. I fought back the tears as her machine started making a loud beeping sound and she struggled to keep her eyes open. I didn't want her to leave this earth feeling like she was a bad person, so I lightly squeezed her hand and poured my heart out to her and cried—something that she had never allowed me to do.

I whispered softly and, through tears, said "Jackie, I don't understand; you never stole anything from me. You always had my back. I can't remember you ever putting your hands on me or raising your voice at me. You allowed me to do things that Nana would never stand for, and that's what makes you special. I wish she were more like you. If I didn't want to go to school, I didn't have to go. I would never forget the time when my school principal called me a bully and you went straight into her office, slapped her face, and removed me from that school. All of my friends thought that was so cool, and they wished that they had a mom like you. I was the only fourteen-year-old in my class who knew how to drive, and that was all because of you. You took me all over the world to some amazing places; we ate at the finest restaurants, stayed in the most expensive hotels, and shopped until our legs got tired." I wanted Jackie to know how much I loved and needed her, so I continued on with these memories for several more minutes, until I noticed that her tears had started streaming down her face at a rapid pace.

I started trembling, and she started squirming as her tears kept right on rolling. I got louder because I wanted her to hear me. "No. You did not steal anything away from me. You gave me opportunities that I would have never had. "Please, Jackie, fight. Fight. Please don't leave me. I need you. I don't want to move away. I want to stay right here with you. I love you."

And just like that, her machine gave a long, steady beep, and then all sorts of doctors and nurses rushed into her room as I started yelling, "No!"

And in the blink of an eye, Jackie took her last breath and slipped away.

REALITY CHECK

It had been two hours since Jackie passed away, and I still hadn't left her side or taken my eyes off of her. The room around me was filled with familiar and unfamiliar voices. Nana sat on the other side of Jackie's bed, inconsolable. We both appeared to be in the same state of mind—stunned.

I heard Uncle Scott drop a few F-bombs after his third attempt to contact Big Man failed. I still couldn't move.

There was a light tapping on the door, and a female voice started to speak in a soft, comforting tone. She offered her condolences, and then she introduced herself as Jackie's head nurse, Olivia Brown. The room fell silent when she respectfully asked for everyone who was not family to please say their good-byes and clear the room so that she could go over some things with the immediate family.

Uncle Scott quickly took charge and asked Nurse Brown to step into the hallway.

I heard the shuffling of feet, long hugs, tears, and good-byes and I still didn't budge as Michael's mom, Debbie, reeking of alcohol, wrapped her arms around my shoulders and whispered, "I'm so sorry," in my ear.

Uncle Scott stepped back into the room and gave a big, heavy sigh. "Mother. Jackson. I need you to find the strength to pull it together; Ms. Brown has something very important to say." *What could be more important than Jackie's passing?* I thought. *There isn't anything that anyone can say to me that will make this empty feeling inside of me go away.*

Uncle Scott called my name again, and for the first time since Jackie had been gone, I took my eyes off of her and focused on him. As I surveyed the room, something didn't feel quite right. Then I realized Big Man was missing. "Where's Big Man? Shouldn't we wait on him?" I asked.

Uncle Scott looked very disturbed when I asked that question. "His wife passed away over two hours ago, and he doesn't even have the decency to answer the phone; that doesn't sound like a Big Man to me. He can go to hell as far as I am concerned," Uncle Scott said furiously.

Nurse Brown hurried and started speaking before any more tensions could build. "Death is never easy, especially when it is a loved one. I met Ms. Jacqueline Scott over fifteen years ago when I dropped out of college and started working at the Lady. Jackie saw something inside of me that I didn't see in myself. She said that I was so much better than that bar. She was the one who pushed me and helped me to get a scholarship so that I could go back to school and pursue my dream of becoming a nurse; and for that, I could never repay her. I loved Jackie, and she was a great inspiration to me."

The Nurse's eyes began to fill with tears as she continued to speak. "Two years ago, when she went to the doctor and he confirmed that the lump she had found on her breast was cancer, she called me. She got a second opinion, and when the results were no different, she decided that she wanted nature to take its course. Chemotherapy was never an option for her; she opted for holistic healing instead. And I can assure you that she did not suffer. We researched and found one of the best holistic doctors the state of Michigan has to offer. He went above and beyond to make sure that she experienced as little pain as possible. He prescribed her with pills and medical marijuana. The pills sometimes caused her to act out and say some things that were not always kind, and the marijuana made her feel relaxed. She said that she never wanted to be a burden on her family, so that's why she confided in me. And after all she had done for me, I was more than happy to be there for her. I would also like to add that it was such an honor to know her, and carrying out her final wish is probably the hardest thing that I have ever had to do."

This lady was starting to creep me out. I had met Jackie's friend Olivia a few times when I was younger, but she was a dancer at the Lady. This high-class lady didn't look like that same person from so many years ago. Besides, if she was Jackie's closest friend, why didn't she know Jackie's last name? Jackie's last name was not Scott; it was Jackson. I didn't know what this lady was up to, but I was going to set her straight.

"Excuse me, nurse; I think I may have heard your name maybe once or twice, but it is very obvious that you don't know Jackie. She was a very private person, and she didn't have any close friends. I'm not sure what you expect to gain from all of this, but a close friend would know that Scott is no longer her last name; it's Jackson."

—

I ignored the embarrassed looks on Nana's and Uncle Scott's faces; I didn't care. This stranger was not going to barge in here and act like she knew Jackie far better than us; we were her family.

I burst out of my seat and yelled "I'm out. I am no longer going to listen to this lady and her nonsense; I need to go and find Big Man."

"Yes, you will listen," Uncle Scott said. "You are being very rude and disrespectful."

The nurse didn't seem bothered by what I had said. She remained professional as she looked at me and said, "You must be Jayson Lee Jackson II, a.k.a. Shorty? I used to change your diapers. Jackie said that you were now more than a handful. Your mother spoke very highly of you, and you were the center of her world."

The nurse reached her hand out to try and comfort me, but I'd had enough of her. I jumped in her face and pointed my finger at her. "If you say one more word about Jackie, I am going to make you eat those words. Make this the last time that I repeat myself: you don't know her!"

Nurse Brown continued to try to remain calm, but she was starting to break. Her voice started cracking as she said, "I know this is hard to accept, but everything that I am about to say to you is in writing, and I gave Mr. Scott a notarized copy."

I eyed the door, praying that Big Man would walk through and send this lady packing; but, as usual, he disappointed.

Nurse Brown continued, and she rose and moved toward a closet as she spoke. "Two weeks ago, Jackie had me meet her down at her attorney's office, where she had her last will and testament drawn up, and she had me make her a promise. She wanted me to see to it that her final wishes were honored." When she finished speaking, she unlocked the closet, reached inside, and pulled out two medium-size boxes wrapped in blue-and-white paper from Tiffany's (one of Jackie's favorite stores). The teary-eyed nurse then handed Nana and me each a box. Mine felt kind of heavy, and I was curious as to what was inside of it. "I would like to finish what I am about to say before you open them," she said with compassion in her voice.

I was growing more irritated by the second. "Are you some sort of guardian angel or something? If so, can you please send Jackie back down here and let her tell us this herself?" I didn't believe anything this woman had to say, and I swear she had only a few more minutes of my time before I ran out of there.

—

She continued speaking, and what she had to say just didn't seem real; it seemed like something you would find in a book or a movie. Uncle Scott stood there looking over the papers as Nana stood there hanging on to hope—hope that Uncle Scott could find some sort of loophole.

The bottom line was, Jackie had died. She knew she was dying, and she had taken care of everything—I mean every last detail. She didn't want a funeral; she wanted a memorial. She didn't want a memorial in a week; she wanted it three days after she died. It was to consist of no more than twenty-five people; twenty-six were too many. She was not a sad person; therefore, her memorial should not be sad—it was to be a celebration. She had the limos, flowers, portraits, food—you name it, she had it covered. She even had a special request: Michael was to sing at the service.

I believe that these requests wouldn't have seemed so bad had she left out the last part; this sent Nana and I both over the edge.

Nurse Brown did as she had been ordered by Jackie (like this was all rehearsed) and told us to open up our presents.

We both opened them up very slowly. When we pulled them out, we saw that they were beautiful matching silver Tiffany vases, and I assumed they had been custom made. I didn't realize that she had had them engraved until Nana read hers:

> I lived, I laughed, I loved, I learned ... I'm Free.
> —Jacqueline Marie Scott

My vase read,

> I will always love you, Shorty.
> —Mom

"No! I won't do it," Nana said in protest. "I will not cremate my child."

I wondered why Nana would say something like that. I thought to myself, *Jackie never said anything about that.* Then, when I observed the object even more, I thought about a movie that I had once seen called *Meet the Parents.* Up on a fireplace in that movie was an urn; it was used to store the cremated remains of the deceased. I realized that this was not a vase; it was an urn. And whether we liked it or not, Jackie was going to be cremated.

Nurse Brown was deeply saddened because Uncle Scott had to console her and Nana both.

Jackie had been very precise with everything, but according to Uncle Scott, she had forgotten one minor detail: she was married, and her name was not Scott, like she had had engraved on that urn. Uncle Scott said Big Man could and probably would contest this, because he was not included anywhere in the will.

Nana's face lit up because she figured she could at least make Big Man give Jackie a traditional burial. That is, until Nurse Brown dropped the final bombshell. She told Uncle Scott to look at the second sheet. He switched the papers around, and he stood silent for a few seconds. Nana and I both looked at him, and that's when he handed the second sheet to us so we could read it for ourselves.

It was a divorce decree. Jackie had divorced Big Man, and it had been final for two weeks.

Nana passed out, and I took off running. I was going to find Big Man and kill him with my bare hands; he was nothing but a no-good user.

MICHAEL (BASKETBALL CAMP)

I had only been at basketball camp for two days when Coach came in and broke the bad news; Jackie had died. He explained everything to me as best as he could. He then told me about her only request: me singing at her memorial. I didn't think that I could do it. I took a seat, because there was no way that I could focus on the game or my skills; this was so unexpected.

My heart went out to Jay and Nana Scott. I really felt sorry for Jay, because I had never witnessed a relationship like theirs; it was truly unique. She was his best friend, and he told her everything. I always envied their relationship; I would never know what it felt like to be loved by the woman who gave birth to me.

I grabbed my towel and my sweat suit and then headed for the locker room; I needed to be alone. I stayed there, praying on my knees for about an hour. I needed to forgive my best friend and be there for him. I asked God to please wrap his arms around the Scott family and take care of Jackie. I got fully dressed, walked back into the gymnasium and asked Coach to take me home; I wanted to be with my grandma and see Nana Scott.

We took the two-hour drive mostly in silence until my cell phone rang; it was Debbie. I had not talked to her since the fiasco at the Scotts'. "Michael, I wanted to see how you were doing." I could tell by the sound of her voice that she had been drinking.

"You know, death doesn't discriminate," I said in a spiteful tone.

"My damn best friend just died; what do you expect?" *No, the heck she didn't just use Jackie's death as her excuse for her drinking.* I thought to myself.

"Just forget it," she said. "Try to make amends with you, and this is the thanks that I get."

I was in no mood for controversy, so I slammed the phone shut.

Hearing Debbie's drunken voice instantly gave me a headache. When Coach caught a glimpse of me rubbing my head, he looked at me with empathy and said, "Do you want to talk about it? We have at least a two-hour drive ahead of us before we reach the city." I didn't answer Coach right away.

Coach had been trying to get me to open up or go and see a therapist to talk about my strained relationship with Debbie for the past few years. Each time, I refused. I accepted the fact that I was never wanted, that Debbie was a substance abuser, and that she hated me. Lately she'd been pushing me to the point of no return, and I was afraid that if I didn't let it out, I might have a mental breakdown.

I looked at Coach, and before I knew it, words started flowing.

"It hurts, Coach," I said with frustration in my voice. Coach eyed me for a quick second before focusing back on the road; I could tell that he hadn't been expecting me to open up. He remained silent as I continued. "She has been putting me down and belittling me my entire life. What did I do to make her hate me so much?" Before I let Coach attempt to answer that question and come to Debbie's defense; I decided to share the most hurtful thing that she had ever said to me. "Coach; do you remember my freshman year in high school, when I placed second in the track meet and got a trophy?"

Coach looked at me and smiled. "Sure I do, Mike. Those boys were all seniors. You did excellent; you only lost by a half of a second. Besides, look how well it paid off; you haven't lost a race since."

"Well, I owe that all to Debbie."

Coach didn't know what to make of what I had just said.

"When I came home and put the second-place trophy that I worked hard for on top of the fireplace, Debbie, in one of her drunken states, fell out laughing. When I asked her what was so funny, she said, "Second place, that's what's so funny." Then she said, laughing even harder, "John Michael, do you know what second place means?" When I didn't answer to that name, she said, "It means you were the first damn person to lose. A ha, ha, ha, ha! You should have come in third. A ha, ha, ha, ha, ha!" I sat there shaking my head, thinking about her wicked laugh, when I caught Coach trying to contain a snicker. "Coach, are you laughing?"

—

He looked at me with water in his eyes, and we both started laughing. Although it wasn't funny at the time, I had to admit that it was pretty funny looking back on it. We were not laughing with Debbie; we were both laughing at her. Coach cleared his throat and said, "Sorry for laughing, Mike; it's just that you have to understand Debbie's personality. When she cleaned herself up years ago, she could tell a good joke. She always made me laugh."

I understood what Coach meant. When Debbie wasn't being mean to me, she was always doing something crazy that made everybody laugh. Like the time last year when she came home drunk and smiling with two missing front teeth. Grandma Betty was appalled. When she asked Debbie what had happened to her teeth, Debbie said that she had fallen, and she then pulled them out of her pocket. Debbie had never come to any of my basketball games, but the day after the tooth accident, she insisted on going. I was so embarrassed as she sat in the front row, toothless, calling my name.

"Mike, you just don't know how good that made me feel, you being able to laugh at that now." Coach said with concern in his voice. "Laughter is very healing."

I looked at him and said "I needed that."

Coach then took the moment as an opportunity to have a therapy session with me. "Whether you like it or not, that's still your mother. Jackie's death really did scare her. She asked for help. She said that she wanted to try to have some sort of relationship with you; she asked me to speak to you."

"It's really not important, Coach; I've learned to suppress it. I guess I just had a moment a few minutes ago."

"Mike, Debbie doesn't hate you," Coach said with a long face. "It's complicated, but I think you are old enough to understand. I have known Debbie for years and sat in many therapy sessions with her. The reason she gave you away was that she was young, scared, addicted to drugs, and lost. When people become addicted to drugs, they don't care about anything but getting that next high. Instead of her trying to leave the hospital with you, she gave you away. She felt you would have been better off with a stranger than with her."

It felt like Coach was pouring salt into an open wound, because I already knew that. I needed to find a way to make peace and move on, so I asked the question that I really wanted to know the answer to. "That was over seventeen years ago, Coach; what about now?"

"Like I said earlier, it's difficult; but I will try. Debbie has a very weak mind, and she knows this. She got addicted to drugs the very first time she tried them. When Ms. Betty made her move back to Michigan, she was able to kick the drug habit, only to pick up a new one—alcohol. She was so afraid that you were going to be weak like her that she treated you meanly. She didn't want you to have the same sheltered upbringing that she experienced, so she did the opposite. She wanted to make sure that you would be able to handle a cold world and stand on your own. She just took it too far."

"What? That doesn't make any sense," I said in a somber voice.

"Michael, I have been telling Debbie that for years. Now that you are doing great, you're strong and you don't need her. She knows that she messed up. Michael, you are everything that Debbie wanted to be. I hate what Debbie has done to you, but I am proud of the man you have become."

"Wow," was all I could say before I leaned my chair back and closed my eyes. Coach turned up the radio and started singing to an old song.

I was just starting to relax when the vibration of my cell phone caused me to open my eyes. The scenery was familiar, so I knew that we were not too far away from home. I looked at my phone and saw that Grandma Betty was calling. "Hello," I said.

She was crying into the phone; I could barely make out what she was saying. I got nervous, so Coach snatched the phone away from me. I heard him say, "Debbie had an accident? What hospital? We're on our way."

LOST

—

I ran through the hospital nonstop; the world was closing in on me. I pushed the elevator button, and when it didn't open right away, I dashed for the stairs and took two and three at a time until I reached the main floor. Once I made it outside, the rain was pouring from the sky. I wondered if the drops were Jackie's tears coming down from the heavens. I turned the corner, leaned against the wall, and threw up. I was a total mess; a lost soul. I pulled out my cigarette and asked a complete stranger for a light; he saw my demeanor and gave me the lighter. I lit the cigarette and inhaled all of the nicotine that my lungs could take; it helped to calm my nerves briefly.

After I finished my cigarette, the rush was back on; I needed to find a ride. That's when I thought about Uncle Scott's driver. I raced up to the car, which was double-parked in front of the building, and tapped on the window. The driver unlocked the door, and I hopped in. "My uncle said to take me home and that you should come back to get him in about an hour."

The driver said, "No problem, sir; he just phoned and informed me about the bad news; you have my condolences." Hearing the word "condolences" put knots in my stomach. I rolled down the window and asked the driver to take me by the bar so that I could locate Big Man. "Who is Big Man?" he asked.

"My fath—the donor."

He asked no further questions.

Ten minutes later we pulled up in front of the bar. The driver rolled down the window and said, "Are you sure this is the place?" I stuck my head out of the window, and I couldn't believe what I was witnessing. The

Lady was getting raided. There were several unmarked black police cars surrounding the whole place; ladies wearing skimpy attire were standing in front of the building, cursing and screaming. A team of guys who were all wearing FBI jackets exited the building hauling pool tables, slot machines, all kinds of liquor, a safe, and several other items.

Finally Big Man appeared. He was wearing shiny handcuffs as he was escorted out of the building by two more men wearing FBI jackets.

"Slow down," I whispered to the driver as if the officers could hear me.

Big Man spotted Uncle Scott's Limo. He saw me. "Shorty!" he called so desperately. It would have been easy to keep on driving like he had done to me, but unlike him, I was no coward. I stuck my head out of the window so that he could know that I saw him. "Tell your uncle I need him to get in contact with my lawyer ASAP!"

He had a lot of nerve; he didn't even have the decency to ask how Jackie was doing. I stared at him with vengeance, and before I knew it, I had flipped him the bird with both fingers. "Pull off," I ordered as I punched the seat in front of me.

COPING

———

Although I wasn't physically homeless, I was mentally homeless. Something was just not adding up. What was the real reason Jackie had divorced Big Man? What could he have possibly done that would make her take such drastic measures? She loved him too much for that. Why did she hide all of that money? Why didn't she take the chemo? Did she not care enough about me to fight? I had all these questions, but no one was there to answer them. I hated my life and I questioned my existence. How could someone have a child and just leave him? I hated Big Man. I had been dealt a bad hand, and I had no idea how to play it.

The driver finally pulled up in front of the house. I was so busy daydreaming that I didn't realize where I was until he got out of the car and opened my door. I asked him if he could keep what we had just witnessed between us; he gave a half smile and nodded.

I got out of the car and walked up to Jackie's brand-new Jeep Grand Cherokee; unlike my life, it was still intact. I went into the backyard and grabbed the shovel out of the shed. I had a feeling that everything I needed to know lay inside that black bag with the gold lock on it.

I dug up the bag and beat the hell out of that lock with my shovel; I took a lot of my anger and frustration out on that lock. After a few minutes, it popped open. I stood there frozen; staring at the bag and all of its contents. I wanted answers; I was just afraid of what I might find.

I decided to take the weed out and smoke a nice fat one to calm my nerves before I went through the bag; my life couldn't get any worse. I took one puff, and already my mind felt like I was in outer space; by the second puff, I was in a whole new world. The nurse was right; that holistic doctor had some of the best weed I had ever had. It really numbed the pain.

———

I started going through the bag, and I counted thirty stacks of bills, each labeled $10,000. Just as Jackie had said; there was $300,000 in the bag. There were several bottles of little pills prescribed to Jackie; I knew those had to be her pain medication. There was an envelope addressed to Jackie from Big Man; it read, "Jackie, you will always be my wife." I opened it. He had left a short note that said "Let's start over," and attached was the deed to the condo that he had purchased for her in his name, along with a set of keys. I still was not satisfied; this was like a jigsaw puzzle, and I was determined to put it together. I kept searching the bag, and at the very bottom of it were two yellow envelopes; one was labeled "Confidential" and the other was from an attorney's office. *Jackpot.*

I re-lit the joint, took a long drag, and popped one of the Jackie's pain pills into my mouth; I was hoping that it would make the pain in my heart go away.

The first envelope that I held was the one labeled "Confidential"; it felt kind of heavy. I ripped it open, and to my surprise, the article that Big Man had done for the magazine fell out, along with a stack of pictures. All of them were of Big Man, a mystery lady, and a young boy who looked to be about seven years old. When I flipped the picture over, I saw that it had been taken eight years ago; this meant that kid and I were about the same age. *Who are these people?* I wondered. There were so many pictures of Big Man with this woman and child, but the odd thing was that they had all been taken over eight years ago. I carefully looked over each picture, one by one, until finally I ran across a newspaper article. It read, "Well-Known Journalist/Children's Author Killed in Head-On Car Collision." Wow. That's why the pictures stopped; she had died. Her name was Carla Roberts, and she had left behind a son. I flipped to the article that Big Man had done for the magazine, and sure enough, he had been interviewed by Carla Roberts. *So that's why he never mentioned me and Jackie in the interview; he was too busy trying to impress this Carla Roberts Lady.*

I opened up the other envelope. In it was a contract with the words "The Lady Too" written across the top. The entire contract had been written up in Jackie's name, and they had left a deposit of $100,000 down with a remaining balance of $200,000 to be paid at closing. When I saw that the contract had been ripped in half that answered one of my questions—Jackie had changed her mind.

—

I had seen enough; I couldn't take it anymore. I grabbed the letters, pills, and weed, along with $500, and tucked them under my arm. I reburied everything else inside the doghouse, where it would stay at least until I could figure out my next move. I headed inside for my room; I needed to pack, because I was getting out of this joint.

I had thrown a few things inside of my duffle bag when the room started spinning. It was a feeling that I had never experienced before; I was delusional. I thought about what the nurse had said about the pills and Jackie's behavior, and that was how I felt—erratic. Then, all of a sudden, I saw Jackie's face. I tried to reach up and grab her, but she soon faded. I started laughing because my mind was playing tricks on me. I couldn't stop laughing as she appeared and disappeared. Then I heard someone whisper my name: "Jaaaaayson, Jaaaaayson."

I answered, but the other person didn't answer back. I started screaming, "Who the hell is there?" Still no answer. I broke out into a cold sweat. I ran to the bathroom and filled the sink up with cold water. As the sink was filling up, I caught a glimpse of myself in the mirror, and I didn't like what I saw; I looked monstrous. My face was beet red, my hair was kinky, my eyes were wide and bloodshot, my nose looked like it belonged on a clown, and my teeth looked like fangs.

The closer that I got to the mirror, the uglier I became. I wanted this feeling to go away, because I was no longer in control; that little pill and the weed were now running the show. I dunked my face in the ice-cold water and counted to ten before I came up for air. "Jaaaaayson," the voice said again, so I went back under for another ten seconds.

When the voice didn't go away, I panicked and ran to Jackie's room. I was going to get rid of the voice forever. I flipped over her mattress and grabbed her gun—the peacemaker. I held it with two hands in the air like Big Man had taught me to do when he had shown me how to fire a weapon last New Year's Eve.

I yelled for whoever it was to come out, but there was nothing but silence. I started looking inside of the closets, in the bathroom, and under the rugs, but no one was there.

With a mixture of water and sweat dripping down my face, I quietly moved toward the stairs. Just then, the door flew open. I pointed the peacemaker straight at the door just as Uncle Scott was entering. I caught myself just in time; I tucked the gun inside my pants before he could see me.

"Jackson, come down here and have a seat; we need to talk," he said sharply and directly. I obliged; I was in fear and in no position to run.

Uncle Scott took one look at my ragged appearance and wrapped his arms around me in pity. "They say the man upstairs puts no more on us than we can handle; I promise we will get through this together."

"How's Nana?"

"Her blood pressure was up. The doctor said it was nothing to be alarmed about. They're keeping her there for observation; she's going to be fine."

Uncle Scott was not his normal self; Jackie's death had taken a toll on him. Every man has his breaking point, and I guess he was no different.

He continued speaking. "It's true; your parents were divorced, and not your father or anyone else can contest her will. That's the way that she wanted it. She made sure that she dotted all of her i's and crossed all of her t's. She even wrote out her own obituary; who ever heard of that?" He giggled slightly. "I have been making phone calls for several hours, trying to see if we can get around this memorial and possibly give her a home going with a burial, but unfortunately we can't. It looks like we will be having a private memorial the day after tomorrow."

"Where does that leave me?" I asked.

"Jackson, you already know. The judge's ruling still stands; after the service, you and Mama are both coming with me to California. She needs to get away for a while."

I tried pleading my case one last time before I took drastic measures. "Please, Uncle, I am begging for another chance. Just let me stay here with Big Man; he bought a new home so that Jackie, he, and I can become a family again." I knew this wouldn't work, especially since Big Man was in jail, but it was worth a shot.

"Where did you get that from? Is that why those boxes are stacked by the back door?" He demanded.

"I found a note; I left it upstairs." I didn't dare tell him about the money and the other contents that now belonged to me. That was none of his business.

"I need to take a look at it." I got ready to run upstairs and grab the paper, but he stopped me. "Wait," he said.

I refused to let him send me through anymore heartbreak. "Uncle, there's probably nothing that you can tell me about Jackie and Big Man that I don't already know. I'm a big boy now, and the only question that you can answer for me is, who are the lady and the child?" I thought to myself, *this is the final missing piece to the puzzle. Jackie has finally outsmarted Big Man after all of these years; she tricked him into letting her handle all of the money for the project, only to bail out. She made sure he would be left with nothing, and I want to know why. If Nurse Brown is who she says she is, I'm pretty sure she filled Uncle Scott in on all the details as to why she did this.*

"How long have you known?" he asked sharply.

"Long enough" I shot back. "Now, are you going to confirm what I think that I already know? Who are they?"

"All right, Jackson, I've contemplated talking to you about this ever since I left the hospital. There's just not a nice way to put it without painting a negative picture of my sister and your father." He took a long deep breath and said, "The truth shall set you free, but they never said that it wouldn't hurt." I braced myself when Uncle Scott said that. He got up and poured himself a drink from Grandpa's liquor cabinet; I had no idea that he even drank.

"If the love of money is the root of all evil, then power has to be a close second. Do you know what that means, Jackson?" I hunched my shoulders in a not-so-sure way. "It means that it is a recipe for disaster. It makes you do whatever it takes to obtain money and power, even if that means hurting the ones you love. It makes you become a selfish person who could care less about morals, values, or consequences." He took another sip from his cocktail. "My sister loved money, and your father loved power; this is the end result." He took one last gulp from the glass before he slammed it down on the table and said, "Now your grandmother and I are left here to pick up the pieces. He went on with his lecture for about fifteen minutes before he told me what I really—but not really—wanted to know.

According to Nurse Brown, it all started right after Big Man and Jackie got married.

* * *

For the first eight years of Jackie and Big Man's marriage, Big Man had a mistress. He had a thing for pretty women, and Carla was definitely his type. She was a journalist who met him when she did a story about him being a young black entrepreneur. They hit it off, and she became pregnant within the first few months, giving birth to their son three weeks before Jackie gave birth to me. Carla was killed in a car accident eight years later, leaving the boy an orphan since she had no known next of kin. The state contacted Big Man so he could establish paternity and gain custody of the little boy, but he refused for fear of Jackie finding out. This caused the boy to be placed into foster care, and from that point on, no one ever knew what happened to him.

Jackie had heard all of the rumors, but she couldn't prove it, and she wasn't really trying to prove it either, because she and I were well taken care of. She didn't want to break up her family, and if she accepted the little boy, that meant she would have to accept Big Man's affair. She chose to put this in the back of her mind. That way she could act like neither the little boy nor the affair existed.

Jackie and Big Man were sitting on top of the world. The Lady was booming, money was flowing, and they were in the process of purchasing a building downtown so they could open up the Lady Too. Jackie and Big Man couldn't have been happier. Then Jackie found a lump on her breast when she was in the shower. She immediately went to the doctor, and he confirmed her fear; it was breast cancer. Once she had gotten a second opinion, her demeanor changed. She said karma had come back around and slapped her in the face. That's when she decided to try and right some of her wrongs.

She went to Big Man and demanded the truth. She said that when she found out that she had breast cancer; a part of her died. She could only imagine how that little boy must have felt after losing his mother. Big Man continued to lie, and this caused Jackie to start despising him, which ultimately made her go out and hire a private investigator. He gave her lots of information: pictures, newspaper clippings, and a few copies of children's stories that Carla had written. But the one thing Jackie wanted was to find the boy, and that was something that the private investigator couldn't produce. The investigator had trouble locating the boy because he had been placed into foster care and later adopted. His name had been changed as well, which made it even more difficult to locate him.

She spent a lot of Big Man's money trying to find this boy, but it never happened. She pleaded with Big Man one final time to help her, and the only thing he said was, "I have no idea what boy you're talking about." That was when Jackie orchestrated a plan, because she was finally going to leave Big Man. She started setting aside her money, took out an insurance policy excluding him, and filed for divorce.

Big Man was angry because things were starting to go badly for him. The FBI was closing in on his illegal activities in the basement of the Lady. The company that he and Jackie had given the $100,000 deposit to for the building downtown wanted to sell the building to someone else for a higher price, making Big Man shell out more money. Plus he had received his divorce papers from Jackie. He knew that he couldn't lose her, because she was the main reason the Lady was so successful. That's why he was trying so desperately to win her back. Jackie never said that she would take him back; she just went along with the plan to be his business partner for the Lady Too because she knew all along that the project would never make it off of the ground; she was just going through the motions.

✳ ✳ ✳

When Uncle Scott shared that story with me, it made me think of the conversation that Nana and Jackie had had years ago. Jackie told Nana that Big Man loved to shine in front of the cameras. She said that it wasn't yet her time to shine. Well, it may have taken her a minute, but I think it is fair to say that Jackie had definitely shined.

Uncle Scott looked at me and said, "Are you satisfied now?"

I was glad that I had answers, but I was far from satisfied. The only thing that went through my mind was that Big Man was one cold-hearted dude, and I didn't like him. I never even bothered to tell Uncle Scott about Big Man's arrest; as far as I as was concerned, justice had been served.

Uncle Scott ended our conversation by adding that he was going to do everything in his power to make his baby sister's wishes come true. He was going to do everything he could to locate the young man Jackie had so desperately wanted me to meet.

Just then his cell phone rang. After a few seconds, he started cursing into the phone as he pointed to the television. I turned it on and saw Big Man walking out of the county jail with his lawyers standing by his side. He had made bail.

Uncle Scott was still cursing into the phone as he grabbed his briefcase and exited through the door without even saying good-bye.

I was so disgusted by the image in front of me that I ran upstairs to Jackie's room and grabbed the keys to both the condo and her jeep. I checked my waist to make sure that the peacemaker was still there as I lit my joint and headed out the door to find Big Man. I needed to settle the score.

Searching For the Truth

In three minutes flat, I was out the door and standing in front of Jackie's truck. It was now dusk and the spring rain had finally let up to a drizzle. I took out Jackie's cell phone and attempted to call Big Man for the fourth time—still no answer.

I opened the back door, threw my duffle bag and the envelopes on the backseat, and took the key to the condo out of my pocket. I contemplated going back inside once I realized that I had left the letter that held the address on my bed, but I got lucky when I searched through the messages on her phone; Big Man had texted her the address four days ago, telling her that she was going to be surprised once she saw what he had done to the place. He had again been trying to buy her love.

When I turned the ignition, I heard loud yelling and screaming, and in a panic I reached for the peacemaker and the door handle, ready to blast whoever was out there. It wasn't until I heard Michael's smooth voice singing that I realized it was only his CD, which was of him supported by some local rap group, playing through the stereo. I was beginning to understand why they say "Don't use drugs"; it drives us crazy. *Note to self: unless I'm planning to end it all, throw those pills away.* Michael's voice was so amazing, and I couldn't understand why he had chosen Basketball over singing; all he needed was a hit record, and he wouldn't have to worry about college or tuition.

I got my nerves back under control and zoomed down the block, headed toward Big Man's pride and joy, the Lady.

I had learned more about Big Man in the previous thirty-six hours than I had in my whole life. Although it hurt, I had no choice but to accept the harsh reality that he didn't give a damn about anything but himself and money. I knew that I could never change that, and at that point, I wasn't sure if I wanted to. The only thing that I wanted from him was help in finding my brother—something that I had always wanted. That was the least he could do.

I pulled in front of the Lady a little after eight, and to my surprise, the place was deserted. The parking lot was empty except for an old black car with a yellow flashing light. It was Mr. Charlie; he was a retired old man who had worked security for Big Man for as long as I can remember. His only downfall was that he loved to drink. According to Big Man, if you bought him a pint of liquor, you had one faithful, dedicated employee. Big man used everyone to his benefit; he didn't even have respect for his elders.

When Mr. Charlie saw me pull into to the bar's parking lot, he got out of the car with his flashlight and walked toward the vehicle. The windows were tinted, so he could not tell who was inside. I rolled down the window, and Mr. Charlie said, "What in the hell?" before he could catch himself. "Shorty, I thought you were Big Man; what are you doing driving this big truck by yourself?"

Not only was Mr. Charlie faithful and dedicated, but he also loved Big Man and would never talk bad or speak negatively about him. "I was looking for Big Man, have you seen him?" I asked.

He stood silent for a few seconds, trying to be selective with his words. "Not since earlier."

I had to let him know that I knew a little of what was going on, because I could tell he was not going to give up anything. "You mean earlier as in when the cops escorted him out of here, or earlier as in a few hours ago when he was released from jail?"

"Hmm. Shouldn't you be at home getting ready for school tomorrow instead of worrying about what grown folks are doing? Now get on out of here; I've got to keep an eye on this place. Everybody's been by here looking for Big Man; I'll add your name to the list." He spoke to me like I was some random stranger instead of Big Man's son.

"Don't mind me, Mr. Charlie; I'm going to hang out here a few in case he shows up." I reached inside my pocket and pulled out a crisp twenty-dollar bill and handed it to him. "Go grab yourself a pint and get me a pack of Newport cigarettes; I will look out until you get back." He had a dumbfound look on his face as he stared at the twenty dollars. I couldn't afford for him to turn me down, so I reached into my pocket and pulled another one out. "Oh, my bad, this should cover it; and keep the change." The dumbfounded look soon disappeared, and he jumped inside of the black car and headed to the store. *Damn*, I thought. *I guess even loyalty has a price.*

I sat in the parking lot for over two hours as several police cars circled the building and at least fifteen people stopped by, all looking for Big Man. He never showed, and Mr. Charlie never made it back with my cigarettes.

I grew tired and gave up. The drugs were starting to wear off, and I was becoming weak and hungry. I was out of weed and cigarettes. The only thing that I had was a pocketful of money, and I had no idea where I could get some more from, since I had left it at home and had no plans of going back there until I found Big Man.

Just as I was about to put the car in drive, a silver Chrysler 300C pulled into the parking lot, right in front of the door. Two young ladies got out of the car wearing long trench coats, stiletto boots, and oversized sunglasses. They both wobbled up to the door and grabbed it like they expected it to be open despite the huge gold padlock on it. They turned around giggling, which made me think they were a pair of bimbos. *I guess you don't have any brains to take off your clothes*, I thought, *because they definitely don't have any.*

Since they couldn't see who was inside of the truck, one of the bimbos, who obviously wasn't used to wearing heels, headed in my direction. As she came closer, I sat straight up in my seat. *Unless the drugs are kicking back in or my eyes are deceiving me, I know her.*

She tapped on the window while her girlfriend stood by the car. I rolled the window down just a little so she couldn't see my face. "Excuse me," she said, "but my girlfriend and I are now ready to try out for amateur night; we went to the spot that you sent us to, and we now have our IDs that say we're eighteen." She gave a little giggle.

It was Kelly, a girl that I had broken up with right before Christmas. She wasn't even old enough to buy cigarettes or beer, let alone dance at a topless bar. Just when I thought Big Man couldn't stoop any lower, I was wrong. He was hiring underage girls to work at the bar. I was glad the cops had shut the place down.

I left the foolish-looking girl standing there as I reflected back on our relationship.

✳ ✳ ✳

Kelly and I had been boyfriend and girlfriend since middle school. Everyone thought that we were the cutest couple. I liked her because she reminded me of Jackie; she was a pretty girl with expensive taste and a bad attitude. All the girls hated her, and all the boys wanted her; but she chose me.

Nana didn't like her; she claimed Kelly was too fast—and she was. She didn't have a problem with skipping school and sneaking up to my room when everyone was asleep; she lived life on the edge, and I loved that about her.

Jackie had only met her a few times; but she adored Kelly. She even said Kelly reminded her of a younger version of herself. So when it was Christmastime and Kelly asked me to buy her a $500 purse, I hollered, "No way."

I told Jackie about it, and she said, "Boy, don't be silly; that's a girl with class." She took me to the mall and purchased the purse, a wallet, and sunglasses for Kelly. They were all Coach brand, and Jackie had them wrapped up with Coach paper and a matching ribbon.

I was so happy and proud of my gift that I stopped by Kelly's house that evening to give it to her. Her mom made me wait in the living room while she went and got Kelly. When I sat down, I couldn't help but notice a smaller box under her tree with the exact same wrapping paper that my gifts were in. I couldn't help but look at the tag, which read, "To Kelly, Love Steve." I was so angry that I opened it. This Steve guy had bought her the matching shoes. I had been played. I threw my present under the tree next to her shoes—because Jackie hadn't raised an Indian giver, and because I was too embarrassed to tell Jackie what she had done—and I walked out of the house and never saw her again.

✳ ✳ ✳

Now here I was, staring at this gold digger in disgust. I never did roll down the window or let her see my face. I revved up the engine really loud and burned rubber right there in her stupid face.

I drove off and pulled into a Coney Island. I sat there in the parking lot and ate my food, and then I typed the address to the condo into the GPS.

The expressway was dark and lonely, and I was ready to fall asleep when the GPS lady said, "Keep straight for twenty miles and exit on Twenty-Three-Mile Road." This was unfamiliar territory for me, so I had to pay close attention to the road, because if I got stopped by the police out there, there was no telling where I might end up.

The GPS lady told me to exit and turn right. She went through directions for several minutes, taking me down winding dirt roads and long streets with no lights. I finally ended up by the lake in front of a row of beautiful condos. This place was definitely low-key, and it was just Jackie's style.

I pulled into the two-car driveway and stared. I didn't know if Big Man had an alarm on the place, but judging by the surroundings, anyone would feel safe there without one. If Big Man were in hiding, this was definitely the place he would come to.

I took out the key and headed up to the door, where I found that there were two stickers with today's date on them from UPS, stating that a first and second attempt to deliver had failed. I knew no one had been there, since the stickers had not been removed. To be safe, I rang the bell, and when no one answered, I closed my eyes and turned the key. The door swung open.

I said a silent prayer for Jackie, and then I opened my eyes. Just like he had promised in his text message, this place was a sight to see. It had tall windows, cathedral ceilings, hardwood floors throughout, and a huge kitchen with an island, and he had rose petals lying throughout the entire house.

I fell to my knees and started crying. I missed Jackie and wanted her to be here.

I thought about the peacemaker that I was carrying and wondered if God would forgive me if I ended my own life. Nothing mattered to me anymore; Jackie was gone, Big Man was missing, and I had a brother out there that I might never get to know. I felt dead anyway.

I made my way to the kitchen, where Big Man had a bottle of Moet Champagne in the refrigerator. I had no interest in drinking champagne, so I opened up a bottle labeled Remy Martin XO—it was Big Man's favorite drink.

Since this would be my first time drinking liquor, I poured myself a tall glass and toasted up to Jackie. I gulped it down in two deep, hard swallows. It burned my insides, making me fall backward as I pounded my chest. I didn't care, so I poured myself another tall glass; I wanted to feel numb, and this alcohol was doing the trick.

Once I was satisfied with the way I was feeling, I grabbed the peacemaker and lay by the front door, waiting for Big Man to arrive.

I had no idea where I was when the ringing in my ears started; it was loud and constant. I was in a state of confusion, and my cell phone started ringing also. My head was heavy, and when I heard someone yelling "Jackson!" through the door, it became heavier. I looked around and had no idea whose place I was in; my memory was gone. I heard "Jackson!" once again and knew who it was—Uncle Scott.

I rolled over. I was extremely intoxicated; this feeling was the worst. I was nauseated and wanted to throw up. The peacemaker fell to the ground, and I picked it up and secured it in my pants. I still heard Uncle Scott's voice; it just sounded so distant. I still couldn't make out where I was or how I had gotten there. I finally picked up my arm, which felt like it weighed a ton, and turned the knob. This would be the worst mistake of my life.

Uncle Scott burst into the home, lifted me up with one arm, and punched me so hard in my chest that he knocked the wind out of me. He then lifted me back up and choked me so hard that his eyes started popping out of his head. My tongue, dripping with saliva, was hanging out of my mouth when he said in an evil tone, "Look at you. You look like a dope fiend, smell like an alcoholic, and are closer to skid row than you can ever imagine. And where the hell is your father? He can come and get some of this too!"

It was then that I figured out where I was. This man was going crazy, and there was no one there to stop him. I looked at him and said, "I don't give a damn; kill me." *At least that way maybe God will let me up into his kingdom,* I thought.

He said, "If I hadn't promised my mother that I would bring you back in one piece, I probably would. I am so tired of you! I have spent so much time trying to save you from your parents, and now I'm trying to save you from yourself. Well, not anymore; your time is up. I don't give a damn what you do. If you want to throw your life away, then that is on you. I will no longer force you to move with me, but I am taking my mother with me, and her house will be off limits. You are pathetic!"

I was waiting on him to tell me something that I didn't already know. I just hoped that he would make good on his promise and leave me alone. He then grabbed me again and said, "Oh, and by the way, you will be attending my sister's memorial, even if I have to drag you there myself." He was mad; and he meant every word of it, because he grabbed my arm, slammed the door, and threw me inside of his limo like I was a piece of garbage.

BROKEN

Suicidal thoughts plagued my mind as the peacemaker rested uncomfortably on my side. My entire body was sore, and I stared out of the window thinking how a single bullet could take me out of my misery. Uncle Scott sat quietly next to me with his head bowed in his hands. I could feel his disappointment and shame. I finally had to admit to myself that I was not only broken; I was shattered.

The limo stopped in front of the house, and Uncle Scott exited the car first. He walked straight ahead, not even glancing back to see if I would run; I guess he had thrown in the towel.

No, I did not run—not that I didn't want to, but because I would never want to let Jackie down, even in death. And besides, it was probably my last hope of seeing Big Man, if he decided to show up.

The door swung open wide, and I was surprised to see that Aunt Sue had made it into town; that made Jackie's death seem more like a reality than the nightmare I wanted to awaken from. She wrapped her arms around Uncle Scott, and I could see that the love and affection they shared with each other was genuine. When they released each other, she focused her attention on me. I hadn't seen her in over a year, and I hated the fact that she was seeing me like this. She appeared to be nonjudgmental, as she grabbed me and held me tight. She wore the same designer perfume as Jackie, and just for a second I got lost in her embrace. She never said a word; she just stood there holding me. Jackie's death had taught me on one thing: no words could take away this pain; it's sometimes best to just say nothing.

I slipped from under her arms and took off for the stairs, hoping that Nana was asleep so she wouldn't see me in my drunken condition. After I showered and got all settled in, I passed out.

The next morning arrived, and it was exactly twenty-four hours until Jackie's memorial. From the sound of it, we had a house full of visitors.

I got my aching body out of the bed, reached inside of my drawer, and pulled out the picture of Carla and the little boy that I had saved. I studied it closely; we both shared Big Man's large eyes and deep dimples. I pulled out a bag of weed and rolled up a joint; I still couldn't believe all that was happening. I hurried to get dressed before anyone had the chance to enter my private sanctuary. The peacemaker was lying next to my pillow, and refusing to get caught without it, I tucked it inside of my jeans.

When I opened the door to my room, Nana was standing there, just getting ready to knock. I felt awkward in front of her, and I couldn't even look her in the eye. I was so happy when she broke the ice and said in her compassionate voice, "I'm so happy that you came back. I've already lost my baby girl; I don't want to lose you." I could have just crawled under a rock and died. "Follow me," she said as she led me to Jackie's room.

Jackie's room looked like a shrine. Grandma had pulled out all of the old photo albums and strategically placed them all over her bed. She had a large oil painting of Jackie and me that Big Man had commissioned on an easel, wrapped and ready to go to the funeral home. Jackie had picked out coordinated beige outfits for us, accented with pink handkerchiefs. Her obituary looked like a beautiful book full of glossy photos from her childhood all the way up until her death. Nana sat there somberly shaking her head. "This is the way she wanted it."

The doorbell continued to ring, and the house was starting to fill up. "Jay, we better get downstairs and start greeting some of these people since they won't be at the memorial tomorrow." I grabbed Nana's hand. I didn't want to see anybody, but it was my only hope of slipping away to get high.

MICHAEL (A CHANGE OF HEART)

My head started pounding. Although Debbie and I didn't have a relationship, I had never wanted anything bad to happen to her. I actually started feeling sad. Even though she was a terrible mother, she was still human; and being human means we all make mistakes.

Our last conversation played through my mind, and I could only wonder—had she really been crying out? My heart went from cold to warm and compassionate in a matter of seconds. I had never been a coldhearted person; I didn't like the energy it brought. So I promised myself that from then on, I would never let a person's behavior change me. Debbie was my mother, and I would love, honor, and respect her no matter what.

I prayed the entire ride to the hospital. I thought about Jackie: *Here today, gone tomorrow. I hope that isn't the case with Debbie.*

We made it down to the hospital just as Debbie was being taken to recovery. The doctor was standing there talking to Grandma as we walked up. "Your daughter is a very lucky woman If you hadn't found her, those pills could have caused severe brain damage and possibly death. We're going to let her rest, but I seriously recommend that she see a psychiatrist and be admitted into rehab as soon as possible."

When he mentioned the words "pills" and "rehab" in the same breath, that told me what I had feared; she had tried to end her own life. This really tore me up, and I didn't want to hear anything further, so I cut him off in midsentence. "Can I please go in and see her?"

He said, "Sure. I just ask that you please keep it brief; she needs her rest."

113

I made it to her room, and she was lying there sound asleep. I stepped up to her bed, and I did something that I had never done before; I kissed the top of her forehead.

She didn't move. I pulled up a chair, picked up the Bible that was lying next to her bed, and turned to Psalm 23, and I softly sang the Lord's Prayer in her ear. She then opened her eyes. It was the first time she ever looked me straight in the eyes. She stared at me for what seemed like an eternity before saying "You are so beautiful."

My heart melted. "Thank you," I said. "I take after you."

She blushed and held back her tears as she said, "I'm going to be going away for a while; would it be okay if I wrote to you?"

I smiled. "How about I go with you and help get you settled in?"

She was elated. "I'd love that."

I sat there for a few minutes, and we talked about Jackie and how we both were going to really miss her. She asked me to sing the Lord's Prayer for her again, and surprisingly, she joined in. I had no idea that she had the voice of an angel. I stopped singing, and she completed the song; it was amazing. Although my visit was short, it was definitely sweet. This was a new beginning for Debbie and me.

MEMORIAL

I stared at the ceiling and realized that today was the day. The final chapter of Jackie's life would be closed. Big Man still had not surfaced, Uncle Scott and I were no longer on speaking terms, and Nana claimed that she wasn't going to California without me.

The house was very quiet. I assumed everyone was in his or her own private space, getting ready to say good-bye. I opened my top dresser drawer to grab my last joint, but I realized that I had smoked it the night before. I felt there was no way possible that I could get through the day without it. I pulled out every drawer and searched all the pockets in my clothes only to come up empty.

Nana called my name from the bottom of the stairs and let me know that the limo would be there in about thirty minutes. I grabbed my clothes and headed for the bathroom, hoping a cold shower would help. I had about fifteen minutes left before the Limo would arrive, and I still had no weed. There was only one alternative left—the bottle of pills that I had found in Jackie's bag. Since I had already taken one before, I knew the effect it would have on me; I was prepared as I popped two into my mouth.

I was getting dressed when I started feeling dizzy. I sat on the edge of the bed and waited until the dizziness went away. Jackie's face once again appeared, but this time I did not try to reach and grab her; I sat there. After I didn't move, her sad face soon faded. That made me feel like I had the high under control, so I grabbed my jacket and the peacemaker and headed downstairs to join the rest of the family.

Everyone was lined up holding hands, waiting on me. I slipped into the line between Nana and Aunt Sue as Uncle Scott led the prayer. The room started spinning, and I started squeezing both of their hands, trying not to fall. "Jay, you're hurting my hand; are you okay?" Nana said in her concerned voice. I started sweating really badly, and Aunt Sue ran to the kitchen to grab a cold towel.

I tried to remain calm and blamed it on my nerves as Aunt Sue patted my forehead.

Uncle Scott said, "It's time," and opened the door.

The morning sun was bright. The birds were chirping, and the four super-stretch Limos made the event appear more like a wedding than a funereal.

Jackie had gone out in style. She had a limo in front of Michael's house, another in front of the Parkers' house across the street, and separate Limos for us. Nana and I both shared our own private limo.

The Limos all pulled down the street one after the other, drawing all kinds of spectators. It was a very sad day, and when I glanced over at Nana, I saw she wasn't looking too good. I wanted to reach out and touch her; however, I was barely hanging on myself.

Several black trucks passed by, and I grew angrier by the second. The drivers all looked like Big Man behind the wheel. I touched my waist to make sure that the peacemaker was in place.

We pulled up to the funeral home along with all the other limos. I started shaking, and the palms of my hands were sweaty. The driver opened the door and helped Nana out of the vehicle first. He held the door open for me, but I couldn't get my legs to move. "Close the door," I said. "I need a few minutes." He did as he was told, and I watched all the others exit their cars and form a single-file line next to the door. Michael and Debbie were the last to exit, and it was strange seeing them hold hands; it really made me emotional.

Everyone entered the building, and I was still hoping Big Man would show.

After about five minutes, I opened the door and exited the vehicle. I heard a loud horn blow, and I turned around hoping it was Big Man. It wasn't.

I opened the door to the chapel, and my eyes grew wide. It looked like an exotic floral shop. Jackie had every type of flower there was. She must have spent a fortune. It was beautiful, as only Jackie would have it.

The Olivia lady walked over and grabbed my hand, trying to guide me to my seat, but I snatched my arm away. I walked over to almost every flower and smelled it. There were collages of pictures of Jackie from the time she was born up until her death; I had never seen anything like this.

I looked around the chapel and counted the chairs; there were exactly twenty-five. All of them were occupied except for two; one was mine, and I assumed the other was Big Man's, since Grandpa was out of the country and I knew he wouldn't make it. It was Just as Jackie had ordered—no more than twenty-five. I had no plans of taking my seat toward the front of the chapel; I needed to be at the back of the church in case Big Man showed up.

Olivia grabbed the microphone and cleared her throat. "If everyone would be seated, we would like to start the celebration now." Uncle Scott looked at me and furrowed his eyebrows, so I found a spot at the back of the chapel.

Olivia started reading the program, and at the end she said that all of the flowers would be donated to the Cancer Institute. Hearing her say that brought tears to my eyes; Jackie cared about making others smile long after she was gone.

Debbie was next to take the podium, and she looked good. She talked about their friendship—the good times and the bad—but overall she talked about how she had loved and admired Jackie.

I kept my eyes pasted on the doors; still holding on to the hope that Big Man would walk through.

Several other people stood up and said many nice things about Jackie that touched my heart, but nothing could compare to when Michael stepped up to the microphone and started singing; he had the entire group in the chapel holding their heads in their laps, in tears.

I tried to contain myself, but I couldn't. I wanted to punch somebody, but the only somebody I could find was the wall. I was hitting it so hard that my fist nearly started bleeding.

The organist began playing louder, which made Michael sing louder, and I could no longer take it. I burst through those doors and turned the corner, and that was when Jackie appeared to me again. This time I started chasing her, and it seemed as though she were crying. I ran until I spotted an empty field. I sprinted to it, fell to my knees, threw my hands up, and started calling her name. She didn't come back.

I pulled out the peacemaker because I wanted to be with her. I started praying to God. "I'm sorry, God," I said. "Please forgive me; I want to be with Jackie." I slowly put the peacemaker up to my head.

Sorrow

———

I had never felt sorry for a person the way that I felt sorry for my best friend. I had been watching him ever since he came into the chapel, and he looked like he was in a daze. I couldn't imagine the pain that he was going through; I had never lost anyone that close to me.

He didn't make eye contact with anyone as he took his time and sniffed every single flower in the chapel. I must admit, it looked like what I imagined the Garden of Eden to be. Jackie was a high-class woman, and this memorial was an exact expression of her life.

Debbie stepped up to the podium and reflected back over all the years that she had known Jackie, sharing some funny, personal, and touching moments. She talked about how their lives had gone into two different directions, but she had never stopped loving her best friend. She even mentioned how Jackie had tried to save her many times, but she just hadn't been ready. She closed out her speech by saying Jackie would be proud to know that she was now ready; she was going to check herself into a treatment facility, and she thanked Jackie for never looking down on her. Her last words were, "I love you, Sis."

I couldn't help but look at Jay at that point, and it seemed as though he were turning pale.

Several more people took the podium, and they had very nice things to say as well. I wanted to walk over to Jay and give him a hug, but then the tall, beautiful lady pointed to me; it was my time to sing.

I kept my eyes on Jay the entire time; he never sat down. The organist started playing. I took the microphone, and once I hit that first note of "Precious Lord," everyone in the chapel started crying. I'd been told that I had a very soulful voice, and it was evident during that song, because there was not a dry eye in the place; women's heads were planted in their laps, and the men were bent over trying to lift them back up. What had started out as a celebration had turned into a sad memorial.

I was still focused on Jay; he was pounding the wall so hard it seemed as though he were trying to knock it down. The organist played louder, which forced me to sing louder, and then all of a sudden Jay burst through the doors and took off running. I dropped the microphone, but the organist continued to play, never missing a beat. I burst through the doors right behind him.

When I ran outside, I didn't see him. I turned the corner, and there he was, on his knees in an empty field, praying up to God with a gun pointed at his head. I didn't call his name, because I didn't want to alarm him; I just took off running in his direction.

I was a few paces away from him, and the entire congregation was emerging from the chapel; they all screamed my name just as I dove over Jay's head.

"Michaellllllllll!"

Bam!

PRESENT TIME........

FORGIVENESS

It's funny how we all seem to live our lives according to what we think God's plan for us is, only to find out we really don't know what his plan is.

For the past two years I have been in rehabilitation therapy, and part of my therapy was to keep a journal. I really didn't see the purpose of this at first, but as I started writing down my feelings, it was very healing for me. Now, as I look back over my life these past few years, I see I have come a long way. I went from bitterness to questioning to acceptance. It was all a part of his plan.

After the accident, the doctors said that I might never walk again. This devastated me and the entire community. Everyone had been so proud of me and my accomplishments; someone from our urban neighborhood was finally going to make it. The devastation didn't last long; they all rallied together and helped me to rebuild my life.

The community, along with the police and fire departments, took up donations, held fundraisers, and never left my side. I had more extended family than anyone could imagine. They made sure all of the house renovations, transportation, and medical bills were taken care of. I must have put on twenty pounds these past few years from all of the homemade meals, cakes, and pies.

Now here I am, sitting in this wheelchair, with the news cameras, my therapist, and my family all waiting patiently on me in the next room. Today is the day that

I will be fitted with my leg braces so I can take my first steps.

To say that I am nervous is an understatement; I am petrified. But through the grace of God, my family, and my friends, I am not alone.

I have been asked many times if I regret sacrificing my life to save a lost soul, and I've always answered no. At some point in our lives, we all will become lost; that still does not make us less worthy. If I were presented with the exact same circumstance today, I can assure you that the outcome would be no different.

I believe that every lesson has a message; it's up to us to accept, embrace, and learn from the message, and that's what I have chosen to do. I no longer focus on the negative; I focus on the positive—and the positive far outweighs the negative.

Had this not happened, my relationship with my Debbie might still be nonexistent. I might have never gotten the chance to do the one thing that I love to do more than anything, even basketball—sing.. I will be releasing my first solo CD in a few weeks; I still can't thank Coach enough for that. And to top it all off, I just completed my sophomore year at Wayne State. I am truly blessed and have no regrets.

P.S. I have no idea how much this letter will impact your decision, but I have forgiven my best friend. The ball is now in your court.

Sincerely,
Michael Stephens

I ripped the letter out of my journal and stared at it for a second, and then I wheeled myself over to my dresser, pulled out an envelope, and addressed it to Judge Kemp; Jay had court in a few days. I took a deep breath and opened the door; my moment had arrived. I had to hold back the tears as everyone in the house gave me a great big round of applause and a standing ovation as I wheeled myself into the room.

The sky really is the limit.

FATE

—

The hour slowly winds down as the recess comes to an uncertain end. Although I feel no closer to my freedom than I did two years ago, this past hour has brought me closer to inner peace. Being on this journey has made me realize so many things: Running away from your past does not change it or make it go away; it only prolongs the healing process. Blaming others for our shortcomings only stunts our growth; forgiveness is essential in moving forward.

As I humbly kneel with my hands clasped together, I can feel Jackie's strong presence. I want to cry, but I can hear her words so clearly: "Shorty, boys aren't supposed to cry." So I dry my eyes. I look up toward the ceiling and I say, "Thank you for giving me life."

I reach inside of my pocket and take out the Dr. Martin Luther King postcard. As I study this strong black man and his powerful words, I look up toward the ceiling, and I apologize to him: "I'm sorry for destroying part of that dream."

After I finish with all of my prayers, my heart is no longer racing. My mind is at ease when the bailiff taps on the door; the hour is finally up. As I am escorted out of the tiny room and the news cameras flash as the news reporters whisper, I am calm.

Everyone is reseated inside the courtroom, and the bailiff once again asks everyone to stand as he introduces the Honorable Judge Kemp. She enters from her chambers with two envelopes in her hands. Uncle Scott appears next to me, and I can tell by his breathing he is nervous. I reach my hand out to console him. "I'm okay," I whisper.

The judge clears her throat before speaking. "Mr. Jackson, now where were we?"

I hold my head up high, and in a very loud, confident tone, I begin to speak. "Ma'am, first I would like to start off by apologizing to Michael. Even though he is not here in this courtroom, I want to personally let him know that I am truly sorry. I love him, and he's always been like a brother to me. I would have never intentionally hurt him. I would give anything to take back that awful day." I am speaking with lots of sincerity and compassion in my voice, and I am praying that Michael is watching. I turn around and look toward the camera and say, 'I love you, man, and I hope that maybe someday you can find it in your heart to forgive me." I then hear a few sniffles and an "Aww."

"The next thing that I want to do is apologize to my nana and Uncle Scott. I'm so sorry for all of the pain, shame, and humiliation that I have put this family through and I want them to know that I take full responsibility for my actions. No one forced me to do drugs, cut school, or pick up a gun; those were choices that I made, and I have suffered tremendously every day for all of those bad decisions."

The judge quickly cuts me off. "Mr. Jackson, please turn around and face your family; I believe they've waited a long time for this"

"Yes, ma'am," I say in a humble voice.

I look at Uncle Scott and say, "Uncle Scott, yesterday you gave me a copy of the letter that I wrote to you the first week that I was here, and I had titled it 'Stolen Opportunities.' He looks at me with a proud grin on his face and nods. "Ma'am," I say, turning my attention to the judge, "I wrote out something last night; would it be okay if I read it?"

She sits straight up in her chair and says, "Of course you may," in a pleasing tone.

I begin reading.

> Missed Opportunities
> I self-destructed at every chance
> of being all that I could be.
> Opportunities that I had
> slipped away from me.
> My mother was a hustler;
> my father was the same.
> I considered myself a victim
> because I needed to shift the blame.
> So many people had tried
> to bring out the best in me;

had I recognized it was tough love,
no telling who or what I'd be.
Then I was dealt a bad hand
that I was forced to play,
and I hated everyone
when Jackie passed away.
My life had changed so fast.
My heart was ripped and torn.
I questioned my existence
and hated the fact that I was born.
But being locked away
has helped me to understand
that making positive choices
will help me be a better man
So if given a second chance
to be all that I can be,
I promise to jump every hurdle
that's thrown in front of me.

When I finish reciting the poem, nearly everyone in the courtroom is in tears. Nana sits there nervously patting her eyes with her pink breast cancer handkerchief. Big Man stands up and abruptly runs out of the courtroom, causing me to lose focus. The judge clears her throat, and by the look on her face, I can tell she is trying hard to hang on to her emotions. "Is that it Mr. Jackson?"

I quickly make myself shake off the negative energy, because my past is now behind me. I no longer want to reach out to Big Man; his running can no longer affect me—I am now immune to it.

"No, ma'am, that's not it," I say in the most sincere voice I can find. "I know that I have a long, challenging road ahead of me, and at times it won't be easy, but I am determined to work hard and persevere through it all." I look at Uncle Scott when I say, "I understand that a path without obstacles probably doesn't lead anywhere. This path that I have been on for the last two years has been a real eye-opener for me. I believe that it saved my life. I promise not to take anything for granted, and I will use this experience as a stepping stone to aim for higher and greater things in life. I also want to give back to the community that I helped to tear down." I think about the small fortune that I have buried, and I know I can make that happen. "I want to mentor other youths and donate my time, money, and anything else that I can to prevent someone else from following in my footsteps. Ma'am, if you let me walk out of here a free man today, I promise that you won't regret it."

"Wow," she says in amazement. "I can't remember the last time I heard something so profound coming from someone so young; very impressive. Mr. Jackson, I want to make you aware that all of this is on record and that the courts will hold you accountable to these words."

"I'm up for the challenge, Your Honor," I say, not wanting to take anything back.

She hands the bailiff one of the envelopes that she entered the courtroom with and says, "Hand this to Mr. Jackson." The bailiff hands me the envelope, and my hand starts shaking when I see that the return address is Michael's. I have no idea what to expect, since I haven't spoken to him in over two years. I wrote him an apology letter a week after I got here, but it was returned by him unopened. I couldn't blame him; he was paralyzed because of me. Nana and Ms. Betty still attend the same church, and they are cordial, but their friendship hasn't been the same since the accident. The judge can tell that I am nervous about opening it, so she says, "Do you need help?"

I take a deep breath and say, "No, ma'am, I can manage."

I close my eyes and say a quick prayer as I open the letter. My heart skips a beat and my eyes start to water as I read the letter from Michael. He has not changed at all; his heart was still made of gold.

The judge looks at me and says, "Mr. Jackson, you really impressed me and the courts today. You are one courageous young man; I respect the fact that you took full responsibility for what you did, and I believe that you learned a valuable lesson these last two years. It's such a shame that some teens never learn how to cope." She says the last sentence in a somber voice, and I know she is referring to Patches. She continues. "You are a strong person, and it's not every day that I receive a letter from a victim forgiving his best friend. If Michael Stephens can find it in his heart to forgive, then the State of Michigan can forgive you also. Mr. Jackson, you are free to go." Her smile appears to be painted on her face.

I can't believe it. I yell, "Thank you, Jesus!" as Nana and Uncle Scott both wrap their arms around me.

We are all still rejoicing when the judge stands up and says, "Oh, I'm sorry, Mr. Jackson, this envelope is for you also. It was addressed to you from Mr. Calvin Roberts before he decided to end his life."

The celebration comes to a standstill as the bailiff hands me the big, heavy yellow envelope. Uncle Scott stands next to me as I rip it open, and out fall several book covers, along with the magazine issue with Big Man in it and what appear to be some old family photos. I don't understand. When I reach over to pick the book covers up, I see they are all children's stories, and the author is Carla Roberts. When I reach over and pick up the photos, I let out a loud cry and I fall into Uncle Scott's arms. They are the same photos that were in Jackie's bag, and those familiar eyes—they were just like Big Man's. Patches was my brother. He even left a copy of his original birth certificate. He was born James Lee Jackson, and Jayson Lee Jackson Sr. was listed as the father; he was born exactly three weeks before I was. It feels like someone punched me in my stomach, and I want to throw up; I am devastated.

Uncle Scott grabs the letter and lets out a loud "Damn!"

We both look around the courtroom for Big Man, but he is gone.

Uncle Scott must be thinking the same thing that I am when he grabs my arm and quickly leads me down the stairs. We both exit into the cold, snowy weather; Uncle Scott goes to the left and I go to the right. I soon spot a cab pulling off with someone with braids in the backseat. "Big Man!" I shout, running behind the cab. I chase it about a half a block before I give up. The cab keeps going. *Big Man still hasn't changed*, I think. *Running is the only thing that he knows how to do best.*

My mind is in a blur as my tears mix with wet snow stream down my face. I head back toward the court building with my brother weighing heavy on my mind. Once I get thirty paces from the building, I spot Uncle Scott talking to a man leaning on the brick wall with one foot propped up, smoking a cigarette. When I get closer, I can clearly see the oversized clothes; the long, nappy dreadlocks; and the raggedy steel-toed boots. It is Big Man. I stop in my tracks and stare.

After I take a long, hard look at him, I realize that though he has been running away for so long, he hasn't managed to outrun karma. It has finally caught up with him; he looks bad. As I inch my way closer, we both focus on each other. Part of me feels hatred, disdain, and disgust; and the other part of me feels pity and sadness for this man who was never taught to love. He spent half of his life trying to have it all; never realizing that he did have it all. Now he has nothing. He has screwed over everything and everybody who ever cared for him, and his clock has finally run out.

As I stand about ten feet away from Big Man, he starts to move in my direction. Suddenly, the heavy snow stops falling, and ironically, the sun starts to shine extremely brightly. I feel Grandpa, Jackie, and my brother smiling down on me. Uncle Scott stays behind and nods his head at me as if to say "It's all right." I know that at this moment, I have to be the peacemaker. I have to let go and forgive, because after reading all of those letters from Grandpa, I understand Big Man better than he understands himself. He can no longer hurt me, and there is nothing that he can possibly give me—my brother is gone—but for the sake of Grandpa and Jackie, I will at least try to be his friend—something that he never learned to be.

About the Author

Author T. L. Criswell is passionate about the well-being of children, and loves writing poetry. She finds that the most effective way for her to communicate with young adults is through poetry. "The Peacemaker" originated from a poem written about a young boy called "Stolen Opportunities" which she self-published in 2008. She works full time in manufacturing and resides in Eastpointe, Michigan, with her husband, son, and adopted nephew.

CPSIA information can be obtained
at www.ICGtesting.com
Printed in the USA
LVOW11s1355091217
559215LV00002B/306/P

9 781458 204981